A Killer Strikes

Georgia Rose

1st Edition Published by Three Shires Publishing

ISBN: (paperback) 978-1-915665-00-3
ISBN: (hardback) 978-1-915665-01-0
ISBN: (eBook) 978-1-9164669-9-9

Edited by Mark Barry
www.greenwizardpublishing.blogspot.co.uk

Proofread by Julia Gibbs
juliaproofreader@gmail.com

Cover design and map by Simon Emery
siemery2012@gmail.com

British Library Cataloguing in Publication Data
A CIP catalogue record for this book is available from the British Library

OTHER BOOKS BY GEORGIA ROSE

The Grayson Trilogy

A Single Step (Book 1 of The Grayson Trilogy)

Before the Dawn (Book 2 of The Grayson Trilogy)

Thicker than Water (Book 3 of The Grayson Trilogy)

The Joker (A Grayson Trilogy Short Story)

The Ross Duology

Parallel Lies

Loving Vengeance

Table of Contents

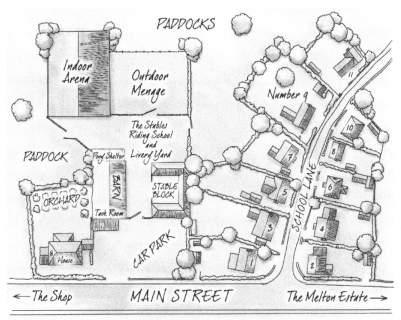

PADDOCKS

Indoor Arena

Outdoor Menage

Number 9

The Stables
Riding School
and
Livery Yard

PADDOCK

Pony Shelter

BARN

ORCHARD

Tack Room

STABLE BLOCK

SCHOOL LANE

House

CAR PARK

11

10

8

7

6

5

4

3

2

← The Shop   MAIN STREET   The Melton Estate →

~ MELTON ~

This is probably not the most suitable book to dedicate to the newest member of the family but hey ho, I can't help the timing. Elsie, you are beautiful, and clever, and strong, and brave. I look forward to spending the rest of my life getting to know you.

Our lives are fashioned by our choices. First, we make our choices. Then our choices make us.

Anne Frank

1: Behold a Pale Horse…

Death is no stranger. I have known it. Tasted it. Seen its violent colours. Its abrupt finality. Yet still, I didn't see it coming. Three days the sheets have hung there. Rain has fallen solidly since yesterday. I ride past the Jacksons' place once again, look over, and there they remain, sodden, clinging to the line, like limp blue sails. It's unlike Jan to have left them out. She runs a tight ship, one that puts mine to shame.

I trawl my memory to see if I can recall her telling me they were going away. She usually would do, as I feed the cats. The faintest whisper of alarm creeps over me. The cats are a fancy, flat-faced, fluffy breed, ill-equipped to provide for themselves. Even now, they could be fading away from starvation. But I come up blank. I always put stuff like that on the calendar. Always. And there's nothing written on it, I checked earlier.

The cars are in the drive. Another sign they've gone nowhere. We last saw them on Boxing Day, but maybe they'd holed up over what remained of the Christmas period. Hibernated away like a sleuth of bears, to watch endless box sets on TV, while they ate their way through multiple snacks and leftover selection boxes. That, I could understand, almost, if it were only John and Jan at home, although it is out of character even for them, but the girls are of an age where they are unlikely to tolerate too much time with the oldies. For instance the eldest, Jenny, has her own car and would surely have wanted to see the New Year in with friends. Yet there it is, in the drive alongside those of her parents and, like them, as far as I can tell, appears not to have moved for several days, the

1

gravel still dry underneath. It makes little sense. Even if they were ill, there would surely have been some signs of life. That thought alone is enough to make me uneasy.

I'm now well past the Jacksons' place, Number 9, and nearly out of the village, so I turn my attention back to Macca. She is one occupant of my livery yard, her owner an Australian. I push her forward into a trot, a pace we keep up for the next hour, to build fitness. Throughout the ride I keep my collar turned against the wind, my face tucked down low to protect myself from the bitter sting of rain coming in on a slant. I slow to a walk for the last half mile to cool Macca down before we get back to the yard.

As I dismount, my eager terrier Scout greets me as though I've been gone for a week. I lean down to scrabble her ears. It's a shame, but I've lost her down one too many rabbit holes, so she can no longer accompany me when I ride out. It isn't worth the worry to come to her rescue so often and I can't bear the thought that one day I might never find her. Now she has to make do with the free run of the stables and adjoining paddocks, scarcely a hardship. As I stand straight again, I roll my shoulders to release the tension built up as I cowered from the elements throughout the ride.

After I put Macca away, I'm kept busy the rest of the morning. Although some owners have shaken off their New Year celebrations and arrived to deal with their own horses, not all have been so keen to brave the filthy weather, so I still have two more liveries to exercise. I've also given Harry and Pip the day off, something I always regret, but know they'll appreciate. This means I still have several more stables to muck out, and the yard duties to do. I'm nowhere near finished when my growling stomach tells me it's lunchtime and, as I've been on the go since six, I need the break.

I cross to the house, Scout at my heels. She sniffs around her food bowl for any surprise treats and curls up in her bed for a snooze. I peel myself out of my wet outerwear, spread my long riding coat over the dryer, and lever my boots off. Then, as the Jacksons have not been far from my mind since the first ride out, when I enter the kitchen from the utility room I glance up at the row of keys to check I still have one for Number 9. I find it buried on the end hook, and my fingers, stiff with cold, struggle to free it from those that rest on top.

'Can I help with whatever it is you're looking for?' interrupts my thoughts and I glance over my shoulder to see my husband, Seb, in the doorway. I finally get the key off the hook and lay it on the windowsill, my intention to pop round to check on the place after lunch. Seb walks further into the kitchen, looking warm and toasty in his thick sweater, the pink pages of his paper folded and held in one hand; the other in his pocket. Clearly, he's had an easier morning than I have, but I know he'll have done something about lunch. I'm not disappointed as he spins the dial on the microwave to heat the soup.

'Thanks, but all sorted. It was the key to Number 9 I wanted,' I say, as he envelops me in a hug, my head tucking neatly under his chin.

Heat radiates off him and I soak as much in as I can, cramming my icy hands up under his armpits, before he grumbles, 'You're freezing.' Stoically, he continues to enclose me in his arms and holds me tight to encourage the heat transfer, one hand wandering lower until it rests on my bottom.

'I know, fortunately I have you around to warm me up,' I say, and with the growling of my empty stomach overriding my

3

need for his warmth, I pull away to run my hands under the tap before I take two large rolls out of the bread bin, split and butter them. "I'm going to go round after lunch, as I'm worried. There's been no sign of them for days.'

'Go round where?' The start of the conversation is already forgotten.

'Number 9.'

'On New Year's Day?' Incredulity is etched into every word. 'They'll have been to a party and are sleeping it off.' I pause. I hadn't considered that. As I think about it, I realise not everyone lives like me with a need for early nights caused by pre-dawn starts. Some people even go out past midnight.

'But the sheets are out. Something's wrong.'

'The what?' His eyes narrow with confusion. I knew that wouldn't make sense to anyone but me. He makes the tea, and I split the soup between our bowls as I explain further.

'Jan has sheets out on the line. She must have hung them out during those bright couple of days after Christmas, but they're still there and it's raining.'

'So, what, you're going to take them in?'

'The sheets? No, well, I might do while I'm there, in case they're ill. Although, you'd think one of them would have been able to have done that.' I mull over this thought as I take the seat opposite Seb and trust the first spoonful of steaming soup rather tentatively to my mouth.

Seb goes quiet and stares into his bowl, deep in thought. He looks over at me with that awkwardly apologetic expression he has when he thinks I won't like what he's about to say. 'You're not going to like this but I don't think you should go round there today.' I meet the eyes of my ever-so-reasonable husband and shrug, because he's right, I don't like it. Knowing me only too well, he peers over his glasses at me, realises he's left them on, and as he hates any outward sign of his advancing years removes them, placing them on the table before he continues in his conciliatory manner. 'They're probably having a quiet family New Year's Day. That *is* what normal people do, you know. Not everyone's like you with dozens of animals to look after so barely gets so much as a lie-in.' His eyes crease pleasantly at the corners as he warms to his theme. 'Some people actually spend the whole day in their pyjamas. They have, what do you call them...?' and he points the half-eaten roll he's holding in my direction as he looks at me, perplexed, as if I would have the answer. I see the look of satisfaction land on his face as he remembers, '... duvet days. Yes. That's what they have. Duvet days.' He dunks his bread, happy he's solved the mystery.

'Hmm, one of those sounds great.' I fantasise for mere seconds on this before I remember I have no patience for such indulgence. I'd manage, maybe, one film under the covers before guilt would drive me back out into the yard.

'That life could be yours, you know?' Seb says, and his eyebrows arch as if it's merely a suggestion when we both know it's not. 'And I wouldn't mind the opportunity to spend a day or two under the duvet with you.' He gives me a cheeky grin, which I can't help but respond to with a smile, but as I continue eating, I return to the problem occupying so much of my thoughts. Much as I hate to admit it, he's probably right. Today might not be the best day to pop in, in case Seb is correct and they are in the middle of a family day, which I'd hate to interrupt. I consider phoning instead, but dismiss that option for the same reasons.

My friends having a duvet day doesn't explain the sheets, though. However, while that continues to puzzle, I realise I've already got plenty to fill my afternoon so, relieved not to have another thing to fit into it, I decide to put off my visit until the next day and change the subject.

'When you haven't been thinking about getting me under a duvet today, what have you been up to?'

'Oh you know, the usual.' I don't know, actually, but as I murmur something to encourage some conversation, he inclines his head towards his newspaper. 'Checking my portfolio, researching potential investments, that sort of thing.'

That sort of thing.

Seb, (called Sebastian by everyone other than me) and I are a case of opposites attracting. As such, we agreed early in our relationship that we would each stick to what we did best. Because he, unbelievably, doesn't like horses, and I don't have the slightest interest in whatever it is he does for a living. Crucially though, we support each other in whatever way we can, and while I'm painfully aware that he does far more for me than I ever do in return, this makes our marriage work.

When he isn't doing his work from home, he works in the City. Something to do with high yield investments and hedge funds. Stuff which I don't fully understand, even though he's explained it to me. Because I have no interest in it, I don't 'get it' as he has said on more than one occasion. A bit like how he'd react should I try to explain the ins and outs of snaffles and pelhams, I imagine. I can see it now, the glazed look forming across his features as he tries not to yawn with boredom.

I leave him to what I suspect will become a doze in front of the wood burner for a good part of the afternoon and wrap up warmly before I venture back outside. Scout jumps up the minute she sees me put on my boots. She's a scruffy brown terrier of indeterminate origin and, as my most faithful of companions, would never let me go to work unaccompanied, however cosy her bed.

As I close the gate to the yard behind me, I smile, surprised to hear a familiar whistle. I know exactly who it comes from. Harry. I turn the corner and can see he's picked up from where I left off. I look in at the stable door.

'I wasn't expecting to see you here.'

'I know, but there's only so much lying around you can do. I need some fresh air.' His Irish lilt is as strong as it was when I first met him many years ago.

'So, you thought what better way to clear the hangover than by mucking out a stinky stable or two?' I grin at him. It's good to see him, and as always I appreciate his help. He knew I would have my work cut out for me today and the sacrifice of his limited free time is the sort of selfless act I've come to expect from him. Harry is an artist. He lives in the self-contained "granny annex" (which he prefers to call a flat) of the old manor house a couple of doors down (although with the houses spaced as they are here, that is some three hundred metres away). I love his art, a lot of it horse related, both paintings and sculptures, but as he's a creative being, his income comes from several sources. He runs workshops and art classes and sells his work through a few different outlets. He also puts in shifts at the local pub, The Red Calf; delivers papers and groceries for the shop on an old rickety bike with a large basket on the front and trailer on the back – and puts in more hours than I pay him for in my stable yard. I'd initially protested when he arrived earlier and stayed later than his allotted shift, because I couldn't afford to pay him for more, but he assured me he was happy to do it. He'd once told me it kept him out of trouble, he enjoyed being around horses and that it was, after all, research for his art. I'd therefore parked the guilt about it long ago and gratefully accepted the extra help.

I shout through from the next stable as I make a start on it, 'Big night at the pub? Did you see in the New Year?'

'Yes…' is his slightly muffled response, '… though I ended up working as Mike was short-staffed.'

'That's a shame.'

'I don't mind the extra, plus it stopped me from hanging today.'

'Good point.' I end the conversation to break open a bale of straw and replenish the bed.

Between us, we make quick work of the rest of the yard. Once the last stable is clean and bedded down with fresh straw, we spend what remains of the afternoon working through the long list of things to do. While it's still light, we go out to the paddocks to check on the ponies. Harry loads up the trailer behind the quad bike with hay nets and while I leap on and off to open and close gates for him, we travel around the fields to check on the occupants of each, hanging up fresh nets and removing empty ones. All the ponies are rugged up and most have had the sense to take cover under the field shelters I had built a few years ago but there are a few I spot, Bassett, Puffin, Smokey and Topaz among them, who prefer to use the hedges for protection, turning their hindquarters into the prevailing wind. Finally, we give them all some hard feed for a much needed winter boost, though Copper comes to nibble at my arm for some affection before tucking in, and I make a mental note to keep an eye on him in case he's going off his food.

8

Daylight has dwindled by the time we get back to the yard. I switch on the lights in the stables, delighted as always to see heads over each of the doors as the occupants wait for us, some more patiently than others. We visit each box to adjust rugs, groom those that need it, top up water buckets and hay nets, before delivering the highly anticipated last feeds. Harry and I work like a well-oiled machine; we've done this together many times.

When all the daily tasks are done, it's already been dark for three hours and I'm back in the house, I send a text to Jan, to wish her a happy New Year. I add, I hope she's okay and raise the possibility I'll pop round tomorrow to catch up. I keep it breezy, like I don't have a care in the world, and wonder why I hadn't thought to have done this earlier. It's such a simple non-intrusive method of contact, but we are low-maintenance friends and as such are rarely in touch outside our planned meet-ups.

I keep my phone by my side.

There's no response.

2: And Death Sat Upon Him

I finish morning stables quickly the next day because of having both Harry and Pip's help, and am back in the house around nine for my second breakfast. I hear Seb on the phone and, because I don't want him to have the chance to dissuade me from my visit to Jan again, I pour milk onto cereal and wolf the lot down as I stand, the bowl held barely below chin level. I put the kettle on to boil for a coffee on my return, then pick up the Jacksons' key and get ready to leave the house, slipping my feet into a pair of tatty trainers. I tell Scout to get back in her bed, adding that I won't be long, then let myself out and hurry along the footpath toward Number 9.

I see Pip on the road up ahead, riding out on her own horse, Pegasus. Otherwise, there is no sign of any other person out and about in the sleepy village of Melton. The rain has stopped, but it's still a drab old day, the sky a grim palette of unrelenting grey. It's a shame because when the sun comes out it lifts the whole place, even in winter the warm sandstone cottages that make up much of the housing here come alive in the light. Today the temperature's dropped as an icy blast is due, and I shiver despite the warm fleece I pulled on for the journey.

The Jacksons live around the corner in School Lane, which is the next road you come to as you travel along Main Road on which The Stables is located. Number 9 is a detached cream-painted house on a plot large enough for a chicken run on one side and John's allotment on the other. The sizeable garden behind backs onto one of my paddocks.

I soon reach the end of the footpath on Main Road and have to take to the road as I turn left into the narrower, and therefore footpath-free, School Lane. While Melton is a quiet village anyway, there's a noticeably more pronounced hush over the place. Ahead, nothing moves but the wind. This only happens at certain times; during the Christmas/New Year break while the schools are closed, and when it snows. Snow always muffles the world. I dwell for a moment on those indulging in a slower start to the day and wonder what it must be like not to have to get up early to tend to animals. To wallow in bed and remain warm and cosy on a day like today has a certain appeal, but it's not something I've ever experienced, having known no other existence than the one I live now. Seb enjoys tempting me with the benefits of such a life, but I don't know if I'd like it.

I hope that I'll see some change in the Jacksons' place. The line bare, perhaps. John about to wash his car. Jan ready to go for a run. My hope is dashed. As soon as I turn into the driveway and come to a halt, I see everything exactly as it had been the day before. John and Jan's cars are in place, steady, reliable models, like the people themselves. Jenny's funky Mini, a fun car, a young person's car, stickers in the back window, also unmoved.

The sheets still hang on the line and although the wind has picked up a fraction, they merely sway slowly back and forth, too wet to billow.

I glance round to see if any of the neighbours are in view. I want to check if there's anyone I can speak to first about my concerns in the hope someone may assuage them before I have to put my key in that lock. There is no one.

I make my way across the gravel. There's a crunch under each step, loud against the stillness of the village, and I'm pleased to reach the porch and the relative silence of solid ground. I ring the bell. Hear its jaunty tune muffled by being

11

this side of the door. I count to thirty. No one comes to answer its call. I prise off my trainers, put the key in the lock and open the door. I take one step into the hall and I know.

They are dead.

My legs weaken, and I take a moment. I bend over, breathe in and out slowly.

Later, when asked, I find myself struggling to explain how I know. But I do. Immediately.

That indescribable essence that makes a house a home is gone.

I consider whether I should leave now and call the police. Take the easy way out. But as I turn towards the door, I imagine the fuss I'll cause if I'm wrong. After all, it's not likely, is it? That they are dead. What if I'm being dramatic? Or overreacting? I'll look a right fool if I call the police and the Jacksons are all tucked up in bed having a lie-in.

A lie-in that's continued despite the doorbell ringing.

I know I have to check first. Because of watching too many crime dramas, I pull my sleeves down over my hands and close the door softly behind me.

As I cut off the flow of fresh air, the smell catches me unawares. Heavy. Metallic. Thick. It cloys in my throat as I pass across the hallway, ignore the stairs for the time being, and check the rooms in order. Kitchen. Utility room – where I find three agitated cats. They leap to the floor as I enter, wind themselves around my legs and mewl. The floor is gritty with scattered cat litter, the trays well-used and smelly. Spotting the empty food bowls, I get their box of dry food out of the cupboard and pour some in each. As they tuck in, I close the door behind me and continue with my tour. Dining room. Sitting room. Study. I open the door to look in the cloakroom, but otherwise touch nothing further. Everything is neat and in order with the usual festive additions of tree, cards and decorations adding an unwelcome clutter I knew Jan would be glad to get rid of in a few days' time.

I circle back to the foot of the stairs and glance up. The metronomic tick of a clock that beats somewhere deep in the house is all I can hear, along with my breaths. I try to slow them, feel my heart pump. Acutely aware of blood coursing through my veins, I hear the thrum of my pulse in my ears. I take a deep breath, then another, and mount the first step.

I've known John and Jan since before the girls were born. Been round for coffee and cake, dinner and drinks. I sat with their babies. Played with their little girls. Helped their teenagers with their angst. I am as familiar with the layout of this house as I am with my own, yet today it feels as if I'm intruding. I reach the top of the stairs; the closed doors make me claustrophobic. I call out their names, my voice weak, and pray for a response.

There is none.

I dread what I have to do next.

I approach the door to John and Jan's room, turn the brass doorknob, then push inwards. My hand springs to my mouth. The smell intensifies. They're in bed. Two heads visible. I call out again in disbelief. My voice quakes. No response. I creep closer, draw level, and reach out a finger and thumb to lift the corner of the duvet gingerly. I gasp behind my other hand, suck in a rapid breath and stagger back as shock drains my body. There's blood. Gallons and gallons of it. Stagnant, murky and in stark contrast to the white of the quilt cover, which I drop. The stench overwhelms and I reel away. I swallow quickly, but to no avail. I vomit cereal into the corner of the room. Then

13

stand and wipe my mouth with the back of my shaky hand, each breath heavy.

The girls…

I look back at the door.

My mouth has dried as I return to the landing and stand outside Judy's room. I force myself to open it and am greeted with violence. Bed covers thrown aside. Judy sprawled face down on the floor, as though downed mid-flight, arms and legs at awkward angles, hair splayed out across a carpet soaked black. A ragged stain spread out from under her body.

I lurch backwards out of the door, rush to Jenny's. Fear constricts my throat as I enter.

She's there. Laid out like Sleeping Beauty awaiting her prince.

There's no blood, but I see marks on her neck. My hand comes to my throat in response.

She looks as though she's merely asleep and although I don't want to, I move closer. I reach out and place two fingers just below the angle of her jaw, seeking a pulse. She's cold to touch, her skin waxy and I know my search is futile.

I turn to leave, sway and sit heavily on the top step of the stairs, my legs unable to take me further.

With an unsteady hand, I take out my phone, dial 999, and try to explain what's happened as coherently as I can. Even as I do so, I feel myself crumble. The words said out loud, making it real. I rock in place. Ragged desperation edges my voice as I plead for help to come. I end the call as tears flood down my face and I let them fall, needing to get them out, to feel their release as I wrap my arms around my body.

I lose myself for a time, then dry my eyes with the heels of my hands. Find a grubby tissue in my pocket to blow my nose. I know it will take an ambulance ten minutes, at least, to get here. There's no rush. There's nothing they can do, but in an effort not to hamper any investigation, I leave the house. I slip on my trainers and sit on the porch step to await their arrival.

My hands shake as I call Seb. Presumably he's still on the phone as it goes to voicemail. This is hardly something I can leave in a message, so I end the call. However, the moment I do so I realise how much I want him here with me so call again, and again, but he's still talking.

The cold works its way into my bones quickly, but I don't have the energy to move. I push away the scenes I've witnessed with difficulty to focus on what needs to be done.

I call Harry and, as I know Pip will be busy with lessons all morning, I ask him to take over my tasks. I consider asking him to go and ask Seb to ring me too, but don't, he's going to have enough to do as it is.

'What's going on? Are you all right?' I hear the concern in his voice, but I don't want to go into it now. There will be enough time for that later.

'I'm fine. Something's happened though that I need to deal with. I'll be back as quickly as I can.' He'll know soon enough it's a major *something* when the police arrive. The news will spread like wildfire through the village. I fear if I talk now, I'll break down again. As long as I know everything is in hand back at the yard, a task he takes on without further question, I can get on and deal with the rest here. I sit, unable to move, and by the time the police car pulls up in the road, I am shivering.

The first two officers to arrive are in uniform. One male, one female. Both young. I stand as they get out of the car. My body, cold and stiff from being in the one position, complains at the movement. They walk over to me. Introduce themselves, display warrant cards, but I take in nothing. I'm asked my details and I explain I made the emergency call. I tell them I found the bodies and gabble on about sheets for a while. A frown comes to the female officer's unlined forehead. She calmly stops me and asks how I accessed the property. I produce the key.

The male officer is already pulling on latex gloves and takes it from my hand.

'You can't do anything to help them,' I say. His jaw clenches.

'I have to check, anyway.'

'They're upstairs.' My voice is quiet. I watch him take a deep breath before he enters. His colleague waits with me. Neither of us speaks as the seconds tick by interminably slowly. When he returns, several shades paler, he makes no reference to what he's seen, but nods to his colleague, confirms, there's no life left to preserve.

She stays with me while he returns to their vehicle. I see him talking into his radio, then he removes a roll of crime scene tape from the boot. The end unravels and, as it twists in the breeze, I read POLICE LINE DO NOT CROSS in blue on white. It's familiar but a television screen has always separated me from it in the past.

I'm distracted from watching him when I'm asked a question. 'You know the householders well, Mrs Percival?'

'It's Laura. Yes, they're friends, I feed their cats," and before I choke again, I give her the family names. She takes down the information in a notebook.

16

'Do you think you could tell me what you did when you went in?' I get distracted before answering as an ambulance draws into the lane. I'm still shivering, unable to stop.

'It's too late for them,' I say. The distress makes me start to cry again and I wipe at my eyes with the back of my sleeve. The officer is sympathetic. She places a hand on my upper arm and tells me it's standard procedure for them to be here. She reminds me of her original question.

Before I get to answer, she asks me to hold on for a moment and stands me to one side while she opens the door in readiness for the paramedics.

When they reach us, she tells them where the bodies are. One, who presumably drew the short straw, enters, and the other speaks to me.

'Hello, can you tell me your name?' She's shorter than me, and younger. A serious face, straight dark hair pulled back into a ponytail.

'Laura.' She smiles kindness.

'Okay, Laura. I'm Joanne. I want to check you over, see that you're all right. Why don't you sit?' I lower myself back down to the step and she crouches beside me.

'I'm fine. I'm not hurt or anything and I need to get home.' She inclines her head as if agreeing, but places two fingers on my inner wrist, concentrates, then withdraws them without comment. Noticing my shivers, she reaches into her bag, pulls out a package and rips it open. Revealing a folded metallic looking sheet which she shakes open before placing it around my shoulders and, as if I've crossed the line in the London Marathon, I clasp the corners of it at my neck with one hand.

'How are you feeling, Laura?'

'Other than cold, fine.'

'Any nausea?'

'No. I've been sick though, in the house,' and I wave my free hand feebly towards the front door. 'Sorry about that.'

'That's fine,' she dismisses my concern. Places the back of her hand against my forehead, then my cheek.

Her partner returns and, after closing the door behind him, quietly confirms all life extinct to the officer. Joanne stands and he asks after me.

'This is Laura,' she says. I smile weakly at him from my seated position. 'She is shivering, so I've given her the blanket. No nausea now, but she tells me she has been sick in the house.' Ridiculously, given the circumstances, I flush with embarrassment. 'Her pulse and skin are fine, and she's answering coherently.'

She turns her attention back to me. 'Any warmer yet, Laura?' I'm surprised that something as flimsy can be so effective as I have stopped shivering.

'Yes, I'm feeling better already.'

'Okay, keep the blanket on for the time being. We'll be over in the ambulance for a while. If you feel worse, come to see us.'

'Can I go home?'

'I think the police will want to talk to you further, first.' I see her glance at the officer for confirmation. She agrees and I wonder how long that's going to take, thinking of all that awaits me back in the yard.

Joanne crouches down beside me again. 'Make sure you rest once the police have finished with you, Laura. You've had a terrible shock and you need to get over that.' Her serious face is back again and I smile my thanks, grateful for her kindness.

Her partner speaks to the officer, says they'll go to report in, and they leave us alone. The officer joins me on the step.

18

'Now, where were we?'

'You wanted to know what I did on entering?'

'Ah, yes. Briefly.'

. 'I checked the downstairs rooms first. I fed the cats but touched nothing else,' I assure her as I explain how I covered my hands. Her eyes narrow.

'So you were already suspicious before you entered the property?'

'Yes, because of the sheets.' I wave a hand weakly in their general direction. Keen to move on past the sheets before I get bogged down in them again, she asks why I'd thought the family were dead. It's not the first conclusion someone would jump to.

'It was the feel of the place.' I'm not sure she would understand if I used words like essence, so leave it at that. Then, as an afterthought, I add, 'Of course there's also the smell,' and I see her grimace. She asks what I did next. I tell her about my time upstairs and apologise for the sick again. I also explain I checked for Jenny's pulse. Then I remember something, sit up straighter.

'Charlie,' I say, loudly. 'Who will tell him? And the rest of the family? Their parents are still alive. They'll be devastated. And their friends…' I tail off. They were so popular, there are many who need to be told.

'Who's Charlie?'

'Jenny's boyfriend. He lives in the village. I'd hate for him to find out through the grapevine.' She makes a note of the details I give her. 'I don't think Judy has a boyfriend. She's a sweet kid, you know?' I can tell she doesn't want to get into all that now. She's going to have her hands full and I see her look up and scan the road for new arrivals.

'We'll deal with informing everyone, don't worry.'

19

She closes her notebook and glances over at her colleague, who has cordoned off the property with tape, extending it out from the corners of the plot to include the width of the verge right up to the road. Another vehicle has arrived, a van, *Police Scientific Support Unit* emblazoned down the side, along with the first of the neighbours, come to see what all the fuss is about. I see the officer at the entrance take details down on a clipboard as he speaks to them.

Another vehicle draws up. Two men get out and the officer with me immediately gets to her feet. These are her seniors. Plainclothes. Detectives. A further police car pulls in behind them.

My officer asks if I can get to my feet. I don't reply, but simply do what I am asked.

'Come on,' she says. 'We should clear the area now it's locked down. The SIO will be here shortly.'

'SIO?'

'Senior Investigating Officer.' She sounds distracted, and keener on encouraging me to move by holding her arm out in the road's direction than on answering my question. Our progress is slow down the drive. Every step an effort now, the gravel shifting under each foot like shingle on a beach. The detectives meet us halfway. I'm introduced and, as with the first to arrive, they give their names, show badges, but I don't take in a word.

The older one of the two tells me I'll need to go to the station. I say I'll go in the morning. He shakes his head.

'I'm sorry, Mrs Percival. You'll have to go now. The officer will take you.'

'It's Laura,' is all I say. I don't protest as, overcome with fatigue, I acknowledge events are out of my control for now.

I'm led to the first police car that arrived and realise it's my officer that's going to take me to the station, which makes me feel even more awkward that I don't remember her name, and it's gone past the point of me being able to ask her for it, again. Her partner joins us and I climb into the back of the police car under the curious gazes of the growing swarm of villagers. The metallic sheet rustles as I sit, then pull the seat belt across to do it up. A wave of exhaustion rolls over me.

My phone rings. It's Seb. I don't want to tell him such devastating news in front of the officers. Some things need privacy, so I turn it off.

3: Carried Along by The Process.

There is silence in the car as we travel to the station. My mind is numb but I find if I try to turn my focus back on to what's happened it's met with disbelief, like I can't acknowledge the reality, so I allow my thoughts to drift again, back to the fuzzy periphery, to protect myself.

At the station, I hand myself over to the process. I'm asked to change out of my clothes, which are taken for potential evidence. I'm given overalls like the ones I saw those that arrived in the *Police Scientific Support Unit* pulling on back at Number 9. They take my fingerprints and my DNA. Despite being reassured these are elimination samples only, because I'd been in the crime scene, I can't help but feel I've done something wrong. Of course, that might be because this is not my first time here. And on the last occasion, I was most definitely guilty.

The blood of a man on my hands.

Despite the horror witnessed earlier, flashes of historical events come unbidden. The setting a trigger. My shame, real and crushing. The questioning, harsh and unrelenting. The grief, raw and all-consuming.

Eventually I'm taken through to a windowless room and asked to wait for the detectives who are to take down my statement. I'm offered a drink and opt for water. For a few moments, I sit in the quiet and appreciate the stillness after the recent blur. They have left me with my phone, but I'm not sure whether to call Seb. I probably should because he's going to wonder where I've gone. If he hasn't already missed me, he certainly will when I don't come in for lunch. However, I can't

22

tell him I'm at the police station without him wanting to know what's going on, and the murder of our friends is hardly news you want to give over the phone. But maybe, villages being what they are, he has already heard that they have taken me away in the back of a police car and will be frantic with worry over what's going on. After this thought, I don't have any choice but to call him.

I brace myself and turn my phone back on. My notifications light up with messages from him. I'm relieved to see there are none from Harry; at least everything is calm in the yard.

I make the call. Imagine Seb snatching up his phone on the first ring.

'Laura! Are you all right? I tried to call you back.'

'Hi, Seb. Sorry, I've only now been able to look at my phone.'

'Why? Where are you?'

'I'm at the police station. I'm waiting for some detectives.'

'Are you okay? What's happened?'

'I'm fine. A bit shaken.' I hesitate, as I try to find the right words. 'I'm sorry, darling, but I've something awful to tell you.'

He's silent on the other end as I break the news as briefly as I can, choking on the words as tears come again.

'Oh my God,' is all he can manage when I finish, his voice tight with shock. 'How awful!'

'I know. I'm sorry to have to tell you like this. You hadn't already heard?'

'No. Been in the office all morning.' He sounds distant, as though his thoughts are elsewhere, and I imagine him trying to get his head around the news. His brow furrowed with worry. 'I'm so sorry, Laura, this is devastating.'

I wipe away tears. 'I can't believe it. Who'd want to do such a thing? You know how lovely they are... were.' This correction causes more tears to flow.

'I do, sweetheart. They were a wonderful family. I can't imagine what sort of animal could do this.' A sadness sweeps over me.

'Say nothing to anyone yet, about what's happened, Seb. The police have said they will put out a statement. I daresay rumours are all round the village already, but I don't want their source to have been me.'

'No, absolutely. I understand.' His voice drifts off again, then he's back. 'Given, er, well, you know, everything, would you feel better if you had a solicitor with you? I can arrange someone.'

I feel a vague sense of alarm at the suggestion. 'I don't think so. I'm not a suspect, Seb. I'm only giving a statement.'

'Of course you're not, but it might be wise to have a legal presence there. A bit of support for you, you know.'

'Thanks, but I'm sure I'll be fine. Like I said, it's only a statement. They want to get it down while it's still fresh,' and I give an involuntary shudder, unconvinced the images I'd seen earlier would ever be anywhere other than imprinted front and centre of my mind.

'Do you need me to do anything? Anything with the yard?' That made me smile. It was so like him. A thoughtful question, but if I'd actually given him a list of jobs that were essential, he'd be completely flummoxed.

'No, that's fine, thanks. I've already spoken to Harry, and that's all in hand.' There's a loaded pause.

'You've already called Harry?'

24

'Yes, I rang you several times, but you were constantly engaged. So I had to call him. I didn't tell him anything about what's happened, but needed him to take over the yard for the day.'

'Of course.'

'I could do with you coming here to collect me later, though, if you could do that, and I'll need some clothes.'

'Clothes?'

'Yes, they've taken mine for forensics. Can you bring me something sensible and warm? I'll call you when they let me out.' The officer reappears with a glass of water. Two men enter the room as she leaves. I'd seen them before, when they arrived at Number 9 earlier. I tell Seb I have to end the call, reassuring him I'll be fine. He's such a worrier where I'm concerned.

The call has been a diversion, and I take a quick sip of water as the two detectives introduce themselves again, only this time I'm in a better state to take in the details. Detective Inspector Ed Pattison and Detective Sergeant Dave Barker. They add they are part of the homicide investigation team.

Homicide. The word sends a shiver through me.

DI Ed Pattison, broad-shouldered, a man built for rugby, is, I'd say, younger than Seb, but has had a harder life. The first suggestion of jowls forming, his skin tired and puffy, furrows at the top of his nose, forged from years of frowning, a permanent feature in an otherwise kind face. Few laughter lines.

He takes a seat opposite and looks over at me. 'So, Mrs Percival—'

I put my hand on the table and move it towards him as I interrupt. 'Please call me Laura.' He inclines his head towards me.

'Laura. I know this has been a terribly distressing day for you, but we need you to give us as much information as you can about the family and what happened today.'

'I'll do whatever I can to help.' Feeling calmer now we've started, I sip at my water. I glance over at DS Dave Barker, who is fiddling around with some equipment. He's younger. Blue eyes set a fraction too close together. DI Pattison tilts his head towards him. 'This interview will be video recorded.'

'That's fine.'

A moment later, DS Barker joins us at the table and they officially introduce themselves again as being present with me for the recording.

'Laura, we're going to come to what happened today, but first, how did you know the Jacksons?'

'I've always lived in Melton and I met Jan and John when they bought Number 9. They still lived in separate homes with their parents until then, I think, but they did some work on the property, got married and moved in. I'd see them around. They had Jenny when I was sixteen and I used to babysit a lot for them. That's when we became friends.'

'How old would they be now?'

'Jan's five years older than me, so thirty-nine, John's forty-one,' I break off when I realise I'm talking about them in the present tense again.

'And the girls?' Pattison prods gently.

'Jenny was eighteen, Judy sixteen.'

'When did you last see any of them?'

'Boxing Day. They always have a big gathering of friends. We went round.'

'That's you and…?'

'My husband, Seb, Sebastian, and Harry and Pip, from the yard. We all know the Jacksons.'

'Did everything appear to be normal?'

'Yes. Jan's a schoolteacher. She was looking forward to having another week off to enjoy the festivities before she had to go back to school.'

'What about John? What did he do?'

'Something at the Council. He was in Planning. I know he'd booked holiday off so he was having a break at home with Jan.'

Pattison tilts his head. Both he and Barker have their notebooks out, despite the recording, but whereas Pattison idly taps at the table with his pen, Barker scribbles down notes intensely. He glances up, and has the look of a ferret, piercing blue eyes, shrewd.

'Did Jan confide in you? Were you close?'

'Yes, occasionally, when we had the chance to catch up.'

'Anything amiss in the family? Matrimonial issues, disputes or arguments?'

'No. They had a happy marriage, and a contented family life.'

'No enemies, rows or disagreements with family or otherwise that you can think of?'

'No. Nothing.'

'And what about the girls? Any concerns there?'

I shrug, 'Other than what you would expect with two teenage daughters, both facing exams this year, no. But no major worries, I don't think.' I pause as Jan's tension on Boxing Day comes to mind. Pattison, astute, notices.

'What is it?'

'Actually, I think Jan was worried about something.'

'Do you know what?' I try to think back.

27

'I sensed she was a bit off on Boxing Day and asked if she was all right.' I pause for a moment, try to remember. 'She looked round like she wanted to see who was in earshot. Then asked quietly if we could meet up for coffee and a chat.' I look down at my hands.

'Who was in earshot?'

'There were a few other friends around, and the girls. I got the impression she didn't want to say anything further in front of them.'

'I take it you didn't get to meet for this chat?' he asks gently, but my face crumples at the thought I hadn't found the time. It's all I can do to shake my head.

'I think whatever was on her mind would have been something to do with the girls. She and John had a solid marriage. I can't remember a cross word between them.'

'She would have talked to you about any issues with the girls?'

'Yes.'

'You were close to them?' A fresh wave of tears pricks at my eyelids and I wipe at my eyes with the cuff of my overalls, the material rough on already sensitive skin. Pattison stretches to reach a box of tissues, which he places in front of me. I pull one out and dab under my eyes, then blow my nose.

'We were particularly close when they were little. I babysat for them a lot. I even went on holiday with them on a couple of occasions to help. But obviously they're grown up now, so I've had less to do with them in recent years.'

'Can you tell me about them? What was Judy like?'

'She was a lovely girl, but feisty too. She knew what she wanted. Good at sports. Bright. Wanted to be a lawyer.'

'And Jenny…?'

28

'She was clever. Predicted to do well in her A Levels. She was planning on taking up a place at Oxford.' I feel a small smile on my lips; I'd been so proud of her.

'What about boyfriends? I understand there is one around, a...' and he glances at his notepad, squints to read what he's written, 'Charlie Button?'

'Yes. He's been going out with Jenny for a while. He's a friendly lad. Lives at the other end of the village.' I give them his address again and add that I don't think Judy was seeing anyone.

'Can you tell me why you went round to the property this morning?'

I explain about the sheets on the line when I rode past and them being there for several days with no sign of the family. I further explain that I'd wanted to go round on New Year's Day but Seb had stopped me, saying they could have been sleeping off the night before. Looking over at the two men, I have to ask about something that has been going round and round in my mind ever since this morning, but still do so hesitantly. 'If I had gone yesterday, would it have made a difference? Could I have saved any of them?'

Pattison shakes his head and looks at me, his eyes kind. 'No, they'd gone well before. There was nothing you could have done.' I breathe out, the weight that worry carried lifted.

'I've been fretting about that since I found them.'

'Do you want to tell me about that? What did you do when you got there this morning?'

I explain my route round the house, how I covered my hands, checked the downstairs first, fed the cats, then went upstairs.

Barker peers up from his notepad, interrupts me. 'It was brave of you to have gone in there at all. For all you knew, the

29

perpetrator could have still been in the house.' A spear of alarm goes through me.

'I didn't even consider that!'

'I don't think that's helpful,' Pattison reprimands his sergeant who, chastened, returns to concentrating on his notebook. The DI looks back at me, a firm set to his mouth. Clearly wanting to gloss over Barker's comment, he asks me to continue. I explain the order in which I found the bodies but don't dwell on what I'd seen.

When I finish, there's a pause. I have to ask, 'Do you have any idea what happened?'

'It's too early to say anything for definite, but can I ask, did you notice anything particular about Jenny?'

'I noticed bruising around her neck.'

'I know this is difficult, Laura. But was there anything else you noticed about that?' I'd gone closer to Jenny than to any of the others, I'd touched her with my fingers, searched in vain for a pulse and clearly seen a row of darker spots around her neck along with more general bruising. I tell them this.

'Okay, Laura. Can I ask you not to say a word about that bruising in particular? We want to withhold some information as part of the investigation.'

'I understand, I won't say a word.' Not that I have any intention of telling anyone anything about the bodies anyway: No one else needs those images in their head.

Pattison sits back in his chair and I sense our time together is ending but he asks again, 'I know we've already covered it, but can you think of any reason why someone would want to kill this family?'

I shake my head. I'm at a loss as to why anyone would want to do this to my friends.

Pattison gets up, the chair scraping on the floor behind him. 'Thank you, Laura. You've been most helpful.' He hands me his card. 'If you have any further information you can tell me or if you remember something later, contact me, day or night. You have my mobile number there.'

'Thank you,' I say, gazing at the card, although not taking in any of the information on it.

'If we have any further questions, we might be back in touch.'

'I understand.'

He and Barker are on the point of leaving the room when he turns back. 'A bit of a warning, too. The media is going to be all over this, so you might need to keep your head down for the next few days. We won't mention your involvement, but you know how word can get out, especially in a close community.'

I feel my stomach clench. This is something I hadn't considered, but I know from bitter experience how tenacious the press can be. Although I'm not close family, I found the bodies and they're all going to want a piece of that.

4: Breaking the News.

As Pattison and Barker leave the interview room my, still unnamed, officer comes in carrying a bulging plastic bag and says she'll take me back to the front desk.

'I have to call Seb to come and get me.'

'No need.' She smiles and holds out the bag to me. 'He's already waiting for you and brought you these.' I take a diversion to the toilets to get changed. Seb had packed jeans and a baggy sweatshirt along with a pair of ankle boots. I'm pleased to get out of the overalls and smile at him with tiredness and relief as I'm taken through to reception. Anxiety is etched across his face and in his hug as he holds me tight.

'I can't believe you've been waiting all this time,' I mumble into his shoulder.

'I came as soon as our call ended. How could I be anywhere else?' His voice chokes and he squeezes me tighter before we separate. He clears his throat and I see him well up as he tries to push his emotions away with practicalities. Holding out the coat he's brought, he helps me into it, takes my hand and leads me out of the front doors. He tells me he's parked up a street opposite the station and I welcome the fresh air on my skin as we walk. The journey home is silent other than when Seb occasionally glances across at me before tentatively asking how I am. I know he's worried and I do my best to reassure him I'm fine even when I'm not sure I am, because I can't bear the look of concern on his face. When we arrive back at The Stables, my inclination is to check to see if everything is all right in the yard, but Seb heads me off. 'Straight into the house, I think. You need to have something to eat.' It is already early afternoon, and we've missed lunch, but it's nausea that gnaws at my insides rather than hunger.

'I'm not sure I can eat anything.'

'Humour me, and at least come and see Scout. She was fretting for you when I left.' That galvanises me into turning towards the house instead of the yard.

There are several cars already in our car park, and a couple who get out of theirs look towards us with curiosity, so I raise a hand in greeting as Seb opens the door. Scout scampers out, wiggling with delight at my return. She takes my full attention as Seb hustles to get us both into the house and out of view. Scout races round the kitchen and sitting room in her excitement, hurtling back towards me for a quick pet before shooting off again in laps.

I hear the kettle heating and as Scout eventually calms I realise I could do with a cup of tea, I shrug off my coat, hang it up and walk through to the kitchen.

'Sit down, Laura. You look like you need to. You're seriously pale.'

'Thanks,' I say, and take a seat at the table, relieved to take the weight off. I feel it. Pale and weak. Drained, I suppose. Emotionally drained.

Seb soon comes over, places a mug in front of me, and takes the chair opposite. He doesn't look too great himself and collapses back in his seat like the stuffing's been knocked out of him. We sit for a moment before he breaks the silence.

'I'm having difficulty processing what's happened.'

'I know, it hardly seems real.'

'I saw the police cars come past, and ambulances. But had no idea where they were going, or that you were involved.' I shake my head. There's nothing I can add to that. He frowns, leans forward in his seat. 'I don't understand why the ambulances would be there if they were all... you know.' He looks away, clearly uncomfortable.

'Standard procedure, I was told. But I saw them, Seb, and they were dead. The only one I thought had any chance was Jenny.' His face brightens for all of half a second, but I dash any hope as I shake my head again.

'They're absolutely sure she's...' but he can't bring himself to say the word. He hasn't known the family as long as I have but he'd got to know them well in the last couple of years as he found out exactly what life and people were like in a small village and enjoyed the big part the Jacksons had played in what amounted to our social circle.

'I checked, and the policewoman and paramedic did, too.' I run my fingers through my hair, then allow my hands to fall back into my lap. They feel too heavy to lift.

'How did they, you know...?' Again he steers clear of the word.

'Jenny looked untouched, other than marks on her neck.' My hand drifts upwards towards mine again. 'I assume she was strangled. The others...' and I shudder. 'There was a lot of blood, but I didn't look that closely. A knife, I suppose. I'm sure we'd have heard gunshots.'

'I'm not sure you would. Not with those sleeping tablets you take.'

'Maybe not, but surely someone would have heard. Someone closer. Anyway, the Scenes of Crime Officers are there, so I guess they'll know soon enough.'

The microwave pings, and Seb rises to answer the call. Moments later, there's a bowl of soup in front of me, buttered bread on the side. I don't think I can face eating, but as he's gone to the trouble, I take a small bite and find after I've swallowed it, my nausea recedes slightly and I take another mouthful. Once started, I manage the rest, clear the bowl too and feel better for having done so. We eat in silence and I'm relieved to see Seb has gained some colour too. Now there's something in his belly.

I look up as I hear hooves coming closer, then see Harry pass by the window on the back of Wooster. He has Candy on a lead rein, so despite Seb urging me to stay put and give myself some time, I finish my tea quickly and get up to go and help him out.

'I'll rest later,' I reassure Seb, and lean in to give him a kiss. For now, there is stuff that needs doing and plenty to keep me busy. And that's what I need, distraction.

Plus, I have to break the news to Harry, because I certainly don't want him to hear it from someone else.

The yard is a hive of activity when I get there as it's lesson switchover time, but I see Pip has everything in hand, so I leave her to it and bypass the mass of ponies to take Candy from Harry. I lead her over to her stable, give her a quick brush down, rug her back up, and take the bridle off.

'Thanks,' Harry says, as he checks over the stable door as he passes by, carrying Wooster's saddle and bridle back to the tack room. 'Everything all right?'

'No. I need to have a word when you have a minute.'

'I've still got to rug Wooster up, so come over once you've finished with her.' He gesticulates with his head towards Candy. I check she has all she needs. Candy is a lovely gentle mare and nuzzles my hand so I give her a bit of extra attention – as much for my benefit as hers – then I leave her stable to cross the yard to Wooster's box to do something I don't want to. Wooster is a huge horse at seventeen hands and it takes a lot of effort to get the rugs up and across his back, a feat Harry has already tackled by the time I get there. I lean on the bottom half of the door and look over.

'So what happened this morning? You okay?' He looks across at me from where he's securing Wooster's rug in place. 'And do you know what's going on down School Lane? It's heaving with emergency vehicles.'

'I'm afraid I have some terrible news that I want to tell you before you hear it from somewhere else.' I open the door and let myself in as he finishes what he's doing and turns to look at me.

'Go on then,' he says, as though bracing himself. Worry lines pucker his forehead and, as I don't know how to soften this, I end up practically blurting it out.

'There's been a tragedy at the Jacksons' place. That's why the police are there. I'm sorry, Harry, they're all dead.' His eyes widen.

'Dead?' He looks bewildered. 'All of them? The whole family? How?'

'It looks like murder.'

'What?' His mouth drops in horror. 'Who by? I thought you were going to say that it was a faulty boiler or a car accident or something. Not murder.'

'I'm sorry, Harry. I didn't know how to say it any better than that.'

'No,' he shakes his head but I can see tears in his eyes, 'No, I can see there's no easy way.' I place my hand on his shoulder and consider giving him a hug if it looks like he needs it.

At twenty-eight Harry is six years my junior and even though he is ten years older than Jenny, I knew she'd had a soft spot for him for years, a feeling I'd long thought he reciprocated.

Because of the age gap, he'd once told me he had done nothing about it but time moves on. They'd occasionally worked at the pub together and appeared to be good friends, so that can often nudge over into something more without too much difficulty. I wasn't sure of the current extent of their relationship. However, whatever it had or had not developed into, I knew Harry would miss her dreadfully. I see tears fill his eyes and he blinks them away as he looks down.

'That's where you were this morning?'

'I'd been concerned, so took the key and went round.'

'So you discovered them? Oh God, how horrible!' Unable to answer, I look away, my eyes filling as I search in my pocket for a tissue.

'Hey,' he says, as he spots my distress. 'I'm sorry, Laura. I know how close to the family you were. You must feel terrible' He places an arm across my shoulders and pulls me to him in a hug.

I sniffle into his shoulder, appreciating the fact I literally had that to cry on.

Seb may be my husband, but Harry is my best friend, and has been for years. He went back to as far as, and beyond, Matt, and the three of us, four on the occasions Harry had a girlfriend, had spent many years socialising together as we'd attempted to grow up. Harry had ended up on our doorstep seeking work, having become a discarded product of the racing yards in Ireland. His dream of becoming a jockey dashed when he grew too tall and broad for the job. He'd fled Ireland at the tender age of eighteen, wanting to start afresh, and ended up in Melton where he developed his second passion, art. He knew what I'd been through and had been there for me every step of the way.

37

Matt was my first husband and the reason I take sleeping pills every night.

I pull away from Harry as I hear the ponies, which I know Pip will lead into the yard after the latest lesson, and we both walk out of the stable.

'Can you let me know when you hear the news from someone else, Harry? I think it's better to let it come out via the proper channels when the police want to share the information rather than us stoking the rumour mill.'

He nods. 'Probably wise. You'd better tell Pip though, and before her next lesson, I heard two parents mention the police activity earlier.' He lifts his chin to indicate in her direction. I see her glance over and can tell from her frown she knows something is up. Some parents follow her gaze, curiosity written on their faces. The problem, as well as the delight, of living in a village is that everyone knows everyone and there is going to be no shielding her from the pain we are all going to face.

'Can you sort out the next lesson? I'll tell her now.'

'Will do.' Harry walks off down the yard as she breaks away and comes towards me, worry tightening her eyes.

'What's up?' she asks brightly, her pretty face upturned towards me from under her riding hat, the dusting of freckles across her nose and cheeks adding to her wholesome, healthy appearance. I indicate for her to follow me into an empty stable.

A few minutes later, following more hugs and tears, she re-emerges drying her reddened eyes but determined to carry on with her next lesson. It's her last of the day for which I'm grateful, as despite us all being workers and therefore knowing our responsibilities and what we have to get done, it's going to be a tough lesson to get through.

Harry gets everyone mounted and Pip leads the new group out to the indoor arena.

When the yard is nearly empty, the parents of the pupils having trailed off behind the line of ponies to watch the lesson from the gallery, Harry comes over. He removes his riding hat and runs a hand through the messy russet mop flattened by it. The dark blue of his eyes stands out against skin that's even paler than it usually is at this time of year. Shock, I suppose.

'Have you spoken to the police yet?'

'Yes. That's where I was this morning. I had to go straight to the station. They took my clothes, fingerprints and DNA, then recorded the interview with me.' His eyes widen.

'Shit. That's heavy.'

'It was, and I think they'll want to speak to everyone who knew the family.'

'That's a long list.'

'Absolutely.' The Jacksons were popular, and, as the most irritating thing about them was the alliteration of their names, I'm still at a loss as to why anyone would want to kill them.

Now that the yard is quiet, a strange sort of paralysis takes over. I can feel any remaining energy drain away as I struggle to focus on what to do next. Harry, of course, notices.

'You get back inside and rest. I can finish here. Pip can help me.'

'Oh no, I can't let—'

'Yes, you can,' he interrupts firmly. 'You're probably still in shock from this morning anyway, so get inside, keep warm, and rest. No arguments,' he adds, when it looks as if I might be going to. I find it difficult to let others cover my work, but I do feel dreadful so agree meekly, thank him, and call Scout to my side as I head out of the yard.

39

5: The Media Are Soon on The Hunt.

Seb is pleased to see me back and ushers me through to the sitting room where I'm told to sit and get comfortable. Attentive to my every need, he's already lit the wood burner, but despite the heat he brings me a blanket, which I snuggle under. I'm so tired I'd like to sleep, but if my eyelids so much as droop, bloody images startle me awake. I gaze blankly into the flames instead.

He brings tea to which he's added sugar, a fact I only discover when I taste it and grimace.

'Hot sweet tea,' he explains, as though I don't understand what it is he's handed me. 'That's what you're meant to have if you're in shock.'

'Are you sure? It's revolting.' But I drink it anyway, to keep him happy, and in case he's right.

He puts the television on and I stare at programmes I've only ever heard about before today. I find myself intrigued by advert breaks filled with mobility devices and stair lifts. Seb fusses around me until I tell him to sit and relax.

He gets out his phone, does precisely that, and I watch him rather than the dire drivel on the box. There's an age gap of fifteen years between us, which he is considerably more conscious of than I am. But he doesn't need to be. Ageing suits men. Seb, better than many. Despite his desk job, he keeps fit at the gym and watches his weight. Those lines that crinkle at the corners of his eyes add a twinkle to his smile. I find the few greys at his temples rather dashing and he is fortunate to still boast a full head of hair that he keeps short to tame the curl. Unlike Harry's pale complexion, Seb tans easily and keeps a healthy colour year round and in direct contrast to DI Pattison earlier, Seb's jawline is firm, his skin taut. He looks after himself, the results show, and it keeps him happy. *Don't want you running off with a younger man,* he'd once joked, and at the time I'd reassured him that would never happen. I don't think he has any idea what a dark place he'd picked me up from, or how grateful I am that he did. You don't simply throw that away.

Harry sends me a text a bit later to tell me the word is out. One of the livery owners had arrived to *supposedly* check in on her horse, something she wasn't known for doing, but it became clear she only wanted to spread the gossip and see if she could learn more. Apparently she wanted to talk to me about the tragedy, as she kept calling it, but Harry had sent her away, kindly but firmly. She is a valued client, after all. He said I was not up for visitors, thank goodness.

Early evening, Seb goes out into the kitchen to put a couple of frozen pizzas into the oven, but makes sure he's back before the news comes on. He sits next to me on the sofa, wraps an arm around my shoulders and holds me close. There's nothing about the murders until the local news. Then we see a stern senior police officer standing in front of the police station I'd been at earlier. It's still light, so this must have been recorded a few hours ago. His title comes up on the screen. He's Detective Superintendent Cooper and I suspect he must be the Senior Investigating Officer I'd heard about this morning. The man in overall charge. I wouldn't want to be in his shoes, and I wonder if he's ever dealt with anything like this before.

Cooper oozes authority as he speaks. In a brief statement, he confirms the attack on a family of four in the village of Melton. No names are given as family are still being informed, and

41

consequently there is no footage of Number 9, but he assures the public of the enormous investment of police resource being made to ensure they find the killer. It ends with a request for anyone with any information to contact the police.

'That doesn't tell us anything we don't know already,' Seb states afterwards.

'I don't think it's meant to. They're trying to control what's put out.'

'What did the police ask you earlier?'

'Only what you'd expect. Preliminary questions about the family, what I did on entering the house, whether I knew of any reason someone would want to do this to them. Stuff like that.' I don't want to rehash it all again, but I tell him what the police said about the likely media interest.

'Don't worry about that. We'll deal with it if it happens.'

I say nothing further, as he won't understand. He wasn't around when Matt died and doesn't know what is about to happen.

Shortly after the news, the phone rings, the Stables' number being easily available. I don't answer, and tell Seb not to either, leaving the calls to go through to voicemail. I hear them though, the messages. All reporters. Local papers. *The Post*. *The Herald*. Nationals. Radio. Television. Exclusives wanted, money offered.

They are quick off the mark. And someone has pointed them in my direction.

I turn off the sound on the landline and pray they don't get my mobile number.

This property is called The Stables. The signage out front reads *The Stables Riding School and Livery Yard* and it belongs to me. The house, which I was born in, the stables and all the

42

associated buildings and paddocks, handed down from generation to generation. I had inherited the property from my spectacularly fearsome mother. In her time, she had added an indoor arena and outdoor menage, with the help of my father's money, to provide herself with the facilities she needed for the life she wanted to live. Unfortunately, her ambition did not stretch so far as to keep my father around for any longer than was strictly necessary and once I had been born she did little to prevent him from straying into the arms of another woman, one who eventually became my wicked stepmother. In fact, my mother barely disguised her jubilation at having got the inconvenience of him out of the way.

My mother was an incredible horsewoman who rode to hounds, competed in high level three-day eventing and, hating the idea of slowing down, took up competitive trail riding in her later years, often covering forty plus miles a day at speed. This was something she did right up until the moment four years ago when an undiagnosed aneurysm burst during a competition, which meant she died as quickly as she had lived.

A force to be reckoned with indeed.

If she was ever disappointed I displayed none of her ambition, and why wouldn't she have been, given all she'd achieved, at least she'd never shown it. At least not directly. At the time, this was something for which I was immensely grateful, as I lacked her confidence. It was only a couple of years after her death that it had occurred to me that our setup had always been exactly as she had intended it. Instead of becoming what I might have been, she had me right where she wanted me as her own personal groom and I had spent years looking after her horses, and Matt's, having been brought up to believe there was only room for one star at a time. She was it for her generation. Matt, she made clear, was it for ours. At least that had been her plan. When that had gone so tragically wrong, something I know she entirely blamed me for too, she was perfectly happy for me to set up my livery business in the yard instead, of course she was, running it, along with her horses, naturally, as I sought to pull something together out of the wreckage of what I'd thought my life would be. It was now obvious to me that was exactly what she had been doing too, keeping me close so as not to lose her support team.

As it is, I now ride well and have gained considerable experience as I spend several hours a day in the saddle, exercising many different horses, each with their own quirks and needs. I have my horse too, Rooster, and compete locally on him. This is all I want, at least, all I want now, and content with the lifestyle I've salvaged, things tick along.

However, while remaining in one place my entire life has brought a certain amount of comfort, I wonder occasionally if I shouldn't have made a different choice, made a fresh start perhaps, as had been suggested at certain times by well-meaning friends in my life. The decision to stay has come to the fore now as recollections fade in and out like ghosts. Every inch of the place so thick with memories they ebb and flow around me like swirling mist. I remember vividly horses that have come and gone, only needing to enter their stable to imagine them there. I can conjure up images such as Matt striding across the yard, my mother schooling a young horse, or Jan at our kitchen table where we'd laugh and chat while sharing a bottle of wine, just as easily. I hope that I've made the right decision to stay, that the good will one day outweigh the bad again. For now, it's all I can do to put one foot in front of the other.

At one point, following a trip to the bathroom, Seb finds me in the kitchen staring at the phone. He gently guides me back into the sitting room and lowers me onto the sofa, tucking me back in under the blanket.

'I'll take care of the messages, don't worry,' he says and I gaze up at him, grateful to have that task taken from me.

Friends call on my mobile and are not so easy to dodge. Everyone knew the Jacksons and all are shocked and grieving. I don't feel like talking, but find I don't have to. I listen. I let them pour out their feelings, so I don't have to let go of mine, and I make sympathetic noises until they burn themselves out. When I've had enough, I put the phone on silent.

The only person I do tell is Maisie Brooks. She, Jan and I were close friends and used to socialise together. Maisie owns one of the large stone cottages opposite my house but is currently living in Spain where she's looking after her ailing parents, and I knew she wouldn't hear the news soon if I didn't tell her. She's also put her cottage up for rent, which is ominous as it shows she doesn't expect to be back anytime soon; a shame as I miss her. Like everyone, she's shocked by the news. We sob together on the phone and I wish she was here so we could hug and mourn as friends should.

The only other call I accept is one from my dad. He spotted the reference to Melton pop up in the online paper he reads and called right away. I fill in the blanks and reassure him. Life has been difficult for him recently, so I don't want to bring more troubles to his door by telling him all about the grim morning I've had. It is enough that he's called, and I appreciate him doing so. Our relationship has been strained and, in truth, practically non-existent for many years because of the previously mentioned wicked stepmother. If I were being honest, it still hurt that he'd chosen to have little to do with me while she was on the scene. (Or maybe it was the other way around. It was hard to tell after all these years.) Whichever, she was now out of the picture. A fact he made me aware of when he called one day a few months ago. Since then we'd made tentative steps to rebuild our relationship, but it wasn't of the sort where he'd drop everything to rush to my side in moments of crisis. Besides, I had Seb for that.

Once the calls are over, I spend the evening continuing to stare at the television, although not taking in what is on, as an unease settles over me which I struggle to decipher. There's an anxious niggle somewhere deep inside that pecks away like a bird after bugs, telling me I've failed to notice something. I try to focus on what that could be but the answer slides away whenever I think I'm closing in on it and I'm left with a constant nagging that there's something I should have done or seen or perhaps a sign I missed that this was going to happen. *Although of course I did, didn't I? Miss a sign.* I look back at the police interview when I mentioned Jan's concern on Boxing Day. I heard that something was wrong, but didn't follow up with Jan for that coffee. What if that could have somehow saved them? What if me not making the time caused this? The questions go round and round without an answer to a single one, and my discomfort deepens as the evening wears on, until the accusation that this is down to me embeds into my bones from where I know it won't shift until it's solved.

I count the hours until I can take my pill. I hope it will bring me respite from the thoughts in my head. Seb stays close but quiet, sensing my mood, and I go to bed shortly after nine.

My sleeping pill successfully blocks out the night, but when I wake to the sound of my alarm, the horror of the previous day floods my thoughts in a rush and I dread what the day will bring.

6: Door-Stepped.

It's all over the national news the next morning, the strapline stark: *Family Murdered as they Slept*. I've been out to do morning stables and now, shortly after eight, I'm back in the kitchen eating a bowl of cereal. Seb calls me through to the sitting room where he's glued to breakfast television. The reporter is in a prime position in front of the fluttering police tape as she fills the audience in on the grim findings within the house behind her. There's something odd about seeing somewhere you're so familiar with on the television and it's difficult to believe this is happening right now, a stone's throw away.

The cameraman zooms in on the flowers laid on the grass outside the property. The village shop must be busy and, as my thoughts turn to Sharon, who owns it, my suspicions rise as to who pointed the press in my direction.

Seb wakes up to the reality of what the next few days will be like when the doorbell rings and he naïvely goes to answer it, despite grumbling under his breath about people who call at this time of day. I hear the door slam and he's back moments later, moaning about bloody reporters.

That was the front door, the one which faces onto the road but which we never use. When I leave to go out to the yard, I'm door-stepped by several reporters at the back door. As I attempt to edge out, with Scout barking and jumping up at the unexpected people in her way, I'm unaware Seb has followed me until I hear his roar.

'This is unacceptable,' he shouts, which makes me jump along with several of the reporters, their hands momentarily frozen in mid-air as they plunge phones towards me to capture whatever gems I'm about to utter.

'Rosie Plankton from *The Post*,' one woman with severe eyebrows perseveres, 'Your local paper, Laura. Don't your friends and neighbours deserve to hear what happened?'

I don't know what happened. Do they think I did? Without waiting for an answer, a man, who didn't even have the decency to introduce himself, calls out, 'What does it feel like to have a murderer living in your midst?'

'What? Who says a murderer is living in our midst?' I mutter as I try to get past him, concerned they've automatically concluded it's someone local, although I guess that would be the natural assumption.

'She has nothing to say,' I hear Seb shout, as I endeavour to make my way through the small group, inwardly cursing whoever spread the word to these vultures. He comes out of the house behind me and, opening his arms wide, starts moving the gaggle of reporters, herding them like reluctant sheep back towards the main gate. I separate myself from the crowd and carry on towards the yard, then see Harry arrive and watch as he joins Seb in removing the reporters from our land.

The main gates are rarely closed, but I watch as the men unhook them from the posts we habitually moor them to, blocking the entrance to the growing number of people congregating on the pavement.

The two men walk over to me. I know there is no choice but can't help saying, 'That's going to cause a problem, because now no one can get into the car park.'

'Let them park out on the road,' Seb says, his annoyance obvious. 'I'm not having you hassled like that.'

'What about getting the horses out on exercise?'

49

'We'll manage,' Harry says. 'I'll come out with you. We'll exercise en masse by riding and leading. That way it will involve as few trips as possible.' Seb approves the plan. We keep our voices low, so no one can overhear, whilst we try to block out the shouted questions coming from the thwarted reporters.

'They'll not be able to ambush you elsewhere either, if Harry's with you. Let me know when you want to leave and I'll open the gate for you.'

Much as I love him, Seb is not normally so willing to involve himself in anything horse related. He made it abundantly clear as soon as we got together that he wanted nothing to do with animals that, as far as he was concerned, did nothing but bite at one end and kick at the other. But I guess desperate times call for all hands to come to the pumps, and I am grateful he's willing to lend his.

'I'll also put some signs on the gate to let everyone know it's business as usual.'

'Thank you.' I smile and place my hand on his forearm as I give him a peck on the cheek. He places his hand over mine, giving it a reassuring squeeze before withdrawing both hand and arm as he turns back to the house. 'Let me know when I'm needed,' he calls over his shoulder.

Harry and I remain; we make eye contact. 'We'd best get on,' I say as we turn as one and, ignoring the ongoing calls from the road, proceed through the yard gate and head for the tack room.

Of the sixteen stables I have, fourteen are currently occupied and all those horses need to be exercised. Pip will ride her Pegasus, and Bertie, who has been on box rest for a month following an operation, will only need to go for a walk around the arena later. That leaves twelve horses to take out, and if

50

Harry and I can each ride one and lead two, we can manage it in only two outings. We rarely do this. The most we will ever lead is one, so this will be challenging, particularly if we don't get the right combinations.

We settle on Harry riding Wooster and leading Macca and Candy, with me on my Rooster leading Pizazz and Sahara for the first session. We tack up, which takes a while, and get organised in the yard, which takes even longer as the horses fuss around with the unusual situation. Fortunately Pip arrives, having struggled to get through the throng at the gate; she tells us, and once we have her to hold our extra horses, the process speeds up. When we are ready, I text Seb and ask him to open the main gate. Pip opens the yard gate wide, and we set off with purpose, me in the lead. Harry and I have had a brief discussion on our strategy and agreed upon the strong, silent approach.

Seb is already pulling open the second half of the main gate. A couple of parents and their children coming for a lesson, taking the opportunity to nip in. I hear him tell the rest of the crowd to keep back, that this was not an invitation. I say crowd. In reality, there are probably ten to fifteen people out there. Some, like Rosie Plankton, are alone, others in pairs like, I notice with alarm, the reporter from the television earlier who appears to be doing a piece to camera right at this moment. I see her glance over at the sound of our hooves coming closer; the cameraman turns the camera to cover us and I deliberately look away as though I haven't noticed and say good morning to our clients instead. I hear Harry do likewise behind me. I hope we will not have to force our way through, but as we get closer we clearly look more intimidating than I feel as the crowd parts like the Red Sea. The road is mercifully clear of moving traffic, so we continue smoothly out onto the highway without hesitation.

It doesn't stop them from calling out their questions, though. They shout over each other, the overlapping confusion battering my ears.

'Laura, how long have you known the Jacksons?'

'Who do you think murdered them?'

'Was it Charlie, Laura?

'Tell us how you felt when you saw the bodies?'

'Why do you think they were killed?'

'What made you think something was wrong at the house?'

I urge Rooster on and keep Pizazz and Sahara close. Once we are clear, I glance back to check Harry is still there and all right. He's presently trying to stop Macca from taking a chunk out of Wooster's neck, but otherwise is fine. I greet his reassuring smile with one in return and press on up Main Street.

The rain may have stopped, but large puddles have formed at the roadside, which are making Pizazz a handful. He hates puddles, is terrified of them in fact, so as I've got him on my nearside each time he shies around them he bashes into my leg. Either that or he hangs back on approach, then cat-leaps them. Both ways he's taking some managing.

I deliberately turn right on leaving the yard as I don't fancy passing the end of School Lane, and certainly wouldn't go down there, so we have a lengthy stretch of road ahead of us before we can get out into the quieter countryside. A few people are about and I greet them all as I ordinarily would, although without my customary smile, which they'll have to forgive in the circumstances. I ignore what I perceive to be their curious glances. But we're definitely attracting more attention than usual. Conversations stop as we approach. People turn to watch us pass. I might be oversensitive but it confirms my fears when we reach the shop and I see Sharon conveniently outside, rearranging and it looks like refilling, the buckets of flowers she has on sale. Her village shop aims to cater to every possible need. From further back up the street, I'd seen her scuttle out of the shop only moments earlier, no doubt a reaction to her hearing the horses approaching, so I brace myself for whatever is about to come out of her mouth.

She straightens her back from her stooped position as we get closer, balls her fists and sets them on ample hips. She waits, brown tabard straining over voluptuous breasts.

'Morning, Sharon,' I say, speaking louder than usual so my voice carries over the sound of multiple hooves on tarmac.

'Morning. You're quite the topic of conversation again, you know?' She says this as if it displeases her.

'Am I? I don't suppose you were the one who told them I was involved, were you?' I slow Rooster's pace.

'Oh! Shouldn't I have done? Didn't realise it was a state secret.'

'It isn't, Sharon. It would just have been thought—' She cuts me off.

'I've had loads of them reporters in here wanting to know all about you.'

I don't ask, but dread what she might have told them. And enjoyed every minute of doing so. Not that it would take much for them to find out, anyway. She hasn't finished. 'Turns out murder's good for business though – we've been rushed off our feet.' *Unbelievable!* I'm past her now and urge Rooster forward again as I aim to get in the last word.

'Every cloud and all that.'

My sarcasm, completely lost on her.

'I was joking with them. It's usually the dog walkers what find the bodies.' She continues calling after us. *She was joking?*

53

I don't look back. But once we're clear, I hear Harry say, 'Nicely handled,' which makes me smile, although I'm not sure that it was.

Sharon is a conundrum to me. In theory, we should get on. We were both born and brought up in Melton and both of us now run successful businesses here. But in practice we don't. Over the years I've been friendly and approachable, but for some reason, one which remains a mystery, she has taken against me, and despite all my efforts in the past I'm now reconciled to the fact we will never be friends.

In fact, rather than even trying to get along, I've always had the impression she loves nothing more than to have something over me and unfortunately my life has provided plenty for her to get her teeth into.

It doesn't help that Sharon, apart from having an incredibly thick skin, is possibly the biggest gossip in the county and someone who sees it as her duty to spread *public information*, as she calls it. Real or fake, she doesn't differentiate. She loves nothing more than being the source. I have absolutely no doubt she will not have held back any snippet about me when the reporters appeared on her doorstep.

The possibility of seeing Sharon was the main reason for not wanting to come this way but, when I'd weighed up the alternatives and assumed she would be busy inside the shop, this route had come out on top. Plus, I did get to confirm that my earlier suspicion about her was right.

We're soon out of the village and I feel I can relax now I'm out from under the spotlight. We turn off into the woods and find an immediate downside to having come out in this ride and lead formation. Generally when out hacking, Harry and I would ride side by side and talk. Doing that has played a large part in us ending up as good friends. However, the paths through the woods are too narrow to manage six horses abreast, so we have to stay as we are. This is a shame as I could have done with the distraction of having him to chat to, especially as I haven't had the chance to ask how he is and he looked terribly pale when he arrived this morning. As it is, I'm left with my thoughts as I push on into a trot, then have to hang on to Pizazz, holding him back as he has a longer stride than either Rooster or Sahara.

'Was it Charlie, Laura?'

That question has been repeating in my head since we left the stables. Knowing Charlie as I do, I'd never considered for one single solitary moment that he would be in any way responsible. Yet that question was being asked, so others must think it. Which meant the police might potentially consider it? It hadn't crossed my mind, when I'd handed his name over, exactly how much trouble I might be getting him into, but then it wouldn't, would it? Because I knew him.

Charlie was in the same year group as Jenny, and I'd known him since he was ten. He helped at the stables on his holidays and occasionally at weekends. That had recently ended because he told me he had to concentrate on his schoolwork. He was aiming at becoming a vet and, somewhat surprised to have been offered a place at university, now had to concentrate fully on getting the highest results possible in his exams.

He hadn't been interested in riding at all, which is unusual in the youngsters who hang around the yard. It was the care of the animals that had always fascinated him. There was something about the way he was with them. His gentle and kind manner, in my mind anyway, ruled him out as being the killer. It simply wasn't possible.

I decide that I'd better mention this to the police when I next speak to them. Give him a character reference, perhaps.

Sahara shies at something, slamming his body into my leg and bringing me out of my thoughts. I check in with Harry, who's doing fine, gather up my reins and try to keep focused.

We're soon on the approach to the stables again. Faces turn towards us as we come into sight and I'm pleased to see Seb heard us coming and has returned to open the gates for us again. He smiles as we pass and I smile back, thankful for his support.

We take a while to get this set of horses cleaned down, rugged up and put back in their stables and the next, and last lot, ready to go out. This time I'll be riding Nebula and leading Henry and Chessington. Harry will have fun on the lively Golden Flame (Flame, for short) and leading Missy and Shades of Grey – stable name Fifty, for obvious reasons.

We go through the same routine as before and I'm glad this will be the last time for today. It isn't the easiest way to exercise and I hope we don't have to continue doing the same for too many days ahead.

My income comes from the horses people keep at livery here. I hope this furore will not put any of them off from coming this weekend as that is when I get a break from all the exercising. However, there are some owners who only come to ride their horse when something special is happening, like hunting or competing somewhere. Some simply don't like the day-to-day exercise, the hacking, the schooling. They like to turn up and have their horse fit and ready for whatever they want to do with it. That's what they pay for.

Other owners keep their horses with us because they work long hours and simply don't have the time to look after them themselves. However, every weekend without fail they will be here to take over the riding and often the other aspects of the care too.

The twelve horses I currently have living in take a lot of looking after. Without Pip and Harry's help, I would be struggling. But they also get a break at weekends and as there are still a few horse-mad youngsters around who turn up to swap mucking out and grooming for riding lessons, that takes the pressure off a degree or two. A lump comes to my throat as I remember a time when Jenny and Judy had been among the kids who helped.

We cross what feels like a picket line outside the stables, the same taciturn expressions on our faces. We engage with no one despite numerous questions being shouted. I notice the television crew has gone.

I turn left this time, not wanting to pass the shop again, and I have to admit I have a certain curiosity to see how much activity there still is outside Number 9. I don't turn down School Lane, but I can see as we pass the entrance the television crew is back outside the police tape again and they are not alone. Other cameras are around and there are vehicles everywhere. I can see several police officers and a couple of people clad, as I was yesterday, in white overalls walking up the drive. We're soon past the entrance and I try to relax by circling my shoulders.

Nebula is a decent horse to ride and one I always enjoy. Liver chestnut, he has a slightly lighter mane and tail which makes it look as if he has highlights. His owner is the nosy one who arrived in the yard yesterday afternoon, but generally isn't around unless it's a weekend, and the sun is shining. A fair weather rider. It's amazing how consistently she calls on a rainy, or cold, weekend, having found she simply has so much to do she can't possibly fit in riding her horse as well.

The two I'm leading are no trouble either, and I take the chance to marvel at the super group of horses I have to look after at the moment. It hasn't always been the case and we've had some proper challenges over the years. Those that have bad stable etiquette, banging doors with their front legs, kicking the walls with their back, chewing the woodwork. Escape artists that slip out given the slightest excuse, one so bad that if you hadn't closed the bottom bolt, he would have the top bolt open and be out should you so much as turn your back on him. We've had biters, and kickers – fortunately rarely – and those that are simply not much fun to ride, especially when you're trying to exercise out with others, because of their antisocial behaviour.

I check back on Harry and he's coping, but I see Flame is already jogging along under him, so I tell him we'll trot on and urge Nebula forward.

I have a couple of empty stables at the moment, which it would be good to fill. Mine is the only livery yard for several miles, so I am often full, but a couple of previous owners are currently between horses, hence the vacancies. There are a few other horses around, though, mostly on local farms but also on the estate. The Melton Estate is on the edge of the village, the bridleway that follows the extent of the external stone wall, one of my favourite rides. I know Emma, who runs the stables for Lord and Lady Cavendish, but not well. We met a long time ago now in The Red Calf and got on, having horses in common. She's since got married to the estate manager, Trent, and they have a daughter, Zaffy. I rarely see her out riding. She's lucky and has the freedom of all the estate land to exercise on, and I'm more likely to bump into her in the village shop than on horseback. She also has a cute terrier, Susie, though I'm not sure how she'd get on with Scout should they ever meet.

We've swapped numbers because occasionally we've helped each other out with spare stables for guests, pieces of equipment or information on local events and competitions, but it surprised me to get a text from her last night. She'd heard what had happened and was offering to help with the yard, horses or anything else, which was incredibly kind of her. I appreciated her contact being by text too, rather than another conversation I would have to steer my way through.

We follow the usual procedure on returning to the yard and I feel much more comfortable once I'm on the other side of the gates, safely on home ground, and know I don't have to go out again. I also feel the morning's been surprisingly productive in the circumstances. I thank Harry for his help.

'Any time,' he says, but he looks tired and distracted as he hoists Flame's saddle up onto its rack in the tack room.

'I'm going in for some lunch soon. Would you like to join us?' I thought he'd accept, as he routinely would do when invited, but he shakes his head.

'No, you're all right. I'll pop back to mine soon.' I leave it there, not wanting to push.

As I approach my back door, blocking out the heckling from the road, I answer a call from DI Pattison. He asks if I can attend the station to go over my statement and add anything further I may have remembered.

'Of course,' I answer. 'I'll come this afternoon. I wanted to speak to you about Charlie, anyway.'

'Oh? What about him?'

'Well, only that I told you about him because he is Jenny's boyfriend, not because I thought he was guilty.'

'You don't think he is?'

'Oh no, it's not in him.'

'It's not in him,' he repeats slowly, as though he's writing down this pearl of wisdom. 'What makes you say that?'

'He's far too gentle. You should see the way he is around the horses.'

'Around the horses?' I can almost hear his eyebrows lift and it occurs to me how bonkers that sounds.

'Yes,' I say, my voice cracking so I have to clear my throat, 'perhaps we could discuss it later?'

'I think perhaps we should,' he says before ending the call and I am left with the distinct impression he thinks I'm a bit of a fool.

7: Someone Close to the Family.

Seb is waiting when I get inside and spots my distraction right away.

'I've had a call from DI Pattison and need to go to the station.'

'What? Right now? Is it an emergency?' His brow furrows.

'No, but I think I've got Charlie into trouble and I need to explain what I mean.'

I pick up my bag from the table, my keys from the bowl on the side, and head towards the back door. Seb beats me to it and raises his hands to slow me down.

'Sit for a minute and take a breath. You've been working all morning and I think you should eat something before you go.' Hesitating, I consider how long I might be out for and reluctantly think he might be right. I can see his relief the moment I turn back to the kitchen, his shoulders relaxing. 'I'll make us some lunch.'

I've become fully aware recently of how many of the domestic jobs he has taken on, certainly more than his fair share. It's come as something of a relief, though. All the paperwork and the finances are now his domain, it being his area of interest and business. Most of the cooking, putting the bins out and, as I apparently don't stack the dishwasher correctly, he does that too, plus he's even gone so far as to put on the occasional load of washing. He's always hung that out though, ever since he moved in and found mould growing on his work shirts because I forget to remove the wet load from the machine, only remembering when I go to put another load on.

61

In fact, the act of hanging out the washing has led to the only thawing there's ever been between him and horse. Bertie, a lovely but at times grumpy livery of ours likes to spend some time of each day outside in a paddock, unless it's bitterly cold. Because he gets on with the ponies that are permanent residents there, Polo, Lopy and Snuffy, I always put him in the one at the bottom of our garden, at the end of which is an orchard. And Bertie does love an apple. Seb was once heard to say, 'When I hang the washing out and take Bertie his daily apple he makes this funny little noise at me.' Sadly, Bertie is grumpier than usual at the moment because he's on box rest and I can't wait to turn him out soon so his mood will mellow.

Moments later, half a loaf, butter and cheese are on the table and I appreciate being able to eat for a few minutes and not have to think about it. He makes my tea strong and I feel better for having taken the time to eat and drink something.

While we are eating, I tell him about the conversation with Pattison and about the things I said about Charlie. How pathetic they must have sounded.

'I'm sure the police appreciate all the information you can give them. It helps them build up a picture.' I find this reassuring. Maybe he's right. 'Do you want me to come with you this afternoon?'

'Oh, no, you're all right.' I hadn't actually considered him coming. 'I doubt you'll be allowed in while I speak to them, anyway.'

'True.'

'And there will be a lot of hanging around if that's the case.'

'I'm not worried about that. I thought it might help to have someone drive you, that's all, and you'd know I was waiting for you.'

I reach out my hand and enclose his with it, giving it a little squeeze. 'You're so thoughtful.' He looks sheepish, as if I've embarrassed him.

'I do my best.' I feel better for having talked it through with him, but decide I will go alone this afternoon. It's not like I'm being questioned as a suspect, after all. It's merely adding to the statement of the facts I've already given. I text Harry to let him know what's happening and to see if he can cover the yard along with Pip until I get back.

I run the gauntlet of reporters. One has the audacity to try the handle and knock on my window as I wait to pull out. I hear Seb yell at him as he closes the gates for me.

Everything is okay until I get to the police station, the driving enough to occupy my mind, but then the nerves set in. I have history here and my foot jiggles as I sit on the hard plastic chair. I cross my legs, but that does nothing to stop it. DS Barker soon comes to collect me and I still my restless foot, but not before his piercing eyes take it in. As I follow him to the interview room, I wonder why the colour scheme is predominantly grey. It must be such a depressing place to work.

I'm offered a drink but decline and DI Pattison joins us only a minute later. The room is small. There's no two-way glass in here and no windows either. My foot jigs again, my entire leg in fact, and I cross my legs once more and force my foot to remain still. I take a deep breath and see Barker's beady eyes on me, and Pattison asks if I'm all right.

'I'm fine. Nervous, I suppose.' I glance around. Yesterday, I was in shock and didn't fully take in where I was or what I was doing. Today, things *are* different.

'Of being in here?' I nod, thinking that was obvious. *Wouldn't anyone be nervous being in here?* But then he comes out with it. 'I see from our records that you have been here before so that's probably why, but there's no reason to be so today. We're only going to run through the events of what happened yesterday to make sure we didn't miss anything and so we have a clear and complete record. You're not in any trouble.' I'd known it would only have been a matter of time before my past was brought up but the fact it has been, and Pattison doesn't seem to feel the need to dwell on it, reassures me. I take another deep breath and try to relax my shoulders that I didn't realise, until now, were hunched.

'If it's all right with you, Laura, we're going to video record this meeting, so we don't miss any of the details. We'll get you to sign it once it's typed up. Is that okay?'

'That's fine.' He indicates for Barker to start the recording. Says the date, time and recounts who's present before he looks back at me.

'So, Laura. I know it's difficult to go through it again, but in case anything else has come to mind, can you tell us what happened yesterday morning, please?'

I do so. Closing my eyes for a moment to centre my thoughts, I take myself back to when my initial concerns were raised and go from there. I explain about the sheets, about Seb advising me against going round on New Year's Day, and about the trip I took round to Number 9 yesterday. Telling them of each place I looked, what I came into contact with, I am detailed. I tell them about feeding the cats, then a thought hits me and I stop.

'What's happened to the cats?' I can't believe I haven't given them a second thought. I haven't gone back to feed them, not that I ever want to go into the house again, but Jan would not have been happy with me. She adored those cats, the thought bringing tears to my eyes once more. How could I have forgotten them?

'We have taken them to a local sanctuary until someone from the family can get here to claim them,' Barker says. 'Why? Do you want to take them in?'

'No. My dog would make their lives a misery. I didn't know if they were still at Number 9 and needed looking after, that's all.'

'We don't leave pets in situations like that,' Pattison says.

'No, no, of course you don't.'

'Shall we continue?' he prompts gently.

I refocus my mind, think about where I'd got up to, and continue. The journey upstairs. The pair of them are quiet, mostly. Occasionally, they prompt for more information, getting things straight in their own minds. I don't give my opinion on anything and they don't ask for it. It is a pure retelling of events and I try to do it as clearly as I can, although once entering bedrooms it becomes difficult and tears fill my eyes, causing pain in my throat. Pattison passes me a box of tissues and asks if I want to stop. I don't, I say, I want to get to the end. He inclines his head and I continue.

I'm shaking by the time I finish. It's harrowing, revisiting, and having to say the words out loud with the pictures so clear in my head. Crossing my arms, I hold them tight to my body as though to warm me. I'm relieved to get it done. I think I did better, gave a fuller account than I'd managed to yesterday.

'Thank you,' Pattison says. 'Would you like a tea?'

'Yes, please. Milk, no sugar.' Barker gets up and leaves the room. Pattison says as much for the sake of the tape, but carries on in his absence.

65

'Are you all right to continue? You can always come back another day.'

'I'm fine.' Although I don't know what there is left to discuss. Barker returns to the room and places a cardboard cup of tea in front of me.

'I'm sorry,' he says, 'it's unlikely to be pleasant.' I expected as much. Don't know why I asked for it. A vending machine cuppa. I smile gratefully and lift the cup to my mouth, but it is far too hot to try yet and I place it back down.

Pattison leans forward, places his forearms on the table, and links his hands together.

'So,' he says, his focus now firmly on me, 'you were telling me about Charlie?'

'Yes.' I try to gather my thoughts again, to make sense. 'I realise I told you about him being Jenny's boyfriend, which may have led you to jump to the conclusion that he did it.'

'We don't jump to conclusions.' His tone is stern.

'No, of course not,' I reply quickly, not wishing to suggest he did. 'I only wanted to clarify that I didn't tell you because I thought he was involved.'

'It is often someone close to the family.'

'I'm aware of that. What I'm saying is that it could be someone close to *another* member of the family.' My glance darts between the pair of them as they look at each other. Pattison returns his gaze to me. I find their interaction interesting. It makes me backtrack, then voice my thought. 'But you already think the violence stems from Jenny, don't you?' Even as a layperson, that had been my assumption, but it did nothing to help Charlie, so I hadn't previously uttered it. Pattison tilts his head.

'I'm more interested in what you think.'

'I think the same.'

'Why?'

'The difference in the deaths, in how the bodies were left.'

'Tell me more.'

'They left Jenny as though on display. She looked untouched, if you forget the bruises around her neck. It was like someone had laid her out to make her look as perfect as possible.' He leans forward so, warming to my theme, I continue. 'I expect they came out of her bedroom and unfortunately were seen by Judy. Her death was much more violent, like they did it quickly, to shut her up.'

'And the parents?' he prompts, 'why would he kill them?' This wasn't so easily explained, but I had one opinion that would discount Charlie.

'Empathy was my first thought. Maybe they are a parent too and know what it would do to them to have lost their daughters?'

'Possibly. Or, he was a friend of the family and didn't want them to suffer. Or,' and he sits back in his chair, 'he simply wanted to tidy up loose ends.' The thought my friends could be considered loose ends horrifies me but I ponder it for a moment. It would make sense to silence them all so they could be sure of a clean getaway. Which prompts another thought.

'Wouldn't the killer have been covered in blood?'

'Undoubtedly.'

'You've said he, once or twice. You're sure a man did this?'

'It's most likely. Jenny had been sexually active in the hours leading up to her death. The autopsy revealed there was semen present. We're awaiting DNA results.'

I'm quiet for a moment while I think. It's careless to leave such damning evidence behind. And it's an unlikely thing to be careless about if someone was planning a murder. Maybe it was an accident? An accident that spiralled into murder.

'Have you questioned Charlie yet?' I reach for the tea again, trust it to my mouth and, as it will no long scald me, take a sip.

'No, we've only recently picked him up as he's been away since New Year's Eve. We're going to interview him once we're finished here.' I hate the thought that Charlie is somewhere in this building right now and probably terrified. I'm temporarily distracted, but then something occurs to me.

'Surely that puts him in the clear. If he was away, he has an alibi.'

'Not exactly. He was only away from the thirty-first. Evidence shows they were probably killed the night before.'

'What evidence?' I drink more tea. Barker was right, and I place it back on the table and push it away.

'Their phones are a good indicator. They were all out of battery. When we recharged them, they sprang to life with multiple messages, yet there was no response from any of the family to any message from the early hours of New Year's Eve onwards.' That is pretty damning. I remember the lack of reply to the one I'd sent and shudder as though someone has walked over my grave.

'You were saying, earlier on the phone...' Pattison reminds me '... about Charlie?' With all the new information, I have forgotten what it was about Charlie I wanted to say to him. 'Something about horses?' he prompts me.

'Ah, yes. It's because he's particularly gentle around the horses.'

'You said that. What do you mean?'

'I mean, Charlie used to spend a lot of time at the stables looking after them.'

'That must be the case for many horse-mad kids?'

'He was different. Charlie wasn't interested in riding at all, purely in the care of them. He liked the grooming, making sure they were comfortable. As he got older, he got involved in their medications and in treating wounds. You know he wants to be a vet?'

'We do.'

'In my experience, people that are kind to animals are generally kind to humans too.' His eyebrows rise like he doesn't believe me. 'I simply can't see him being responsible for anything so... so... barbaric.' Pattison takes a few moments to consider my words.

'I'll take your thoughts on board, Laura. But I think you'd be surprised by what people can do. I daresay there have been a fair few killers out there who loved their pets.'

'I'm sure, but he has always appeared to be such an innocent in life and he and Jenny were so close. It's not like they had a stormy relationship or anything.' I knew things could turn on a sixpence, but even if they ever rowed, I couldn't imagine Charlie getting violent. If anything, he was probably the gentler of the two of them and more laid back about life. Whereas I knew Jenny was a strong young woman. Even as a child, she'd known exactly what she wanted and had the determination to get it. Pattison leans on the table again.

'You've put a lot of thought into this.'

'Obviously. I can't get it out of my mind.' Little else has consumed my thoughts since discovering the bodies. The questions that whirl through my brain like tumbling clothes in a dryer exhaust me.

'I understand.' He takes a breath, 'Look, Laura. Our investigations are at an early stage, and are continuing, even though it may look like we have someone of interest. We'll take your thoughts on Charlie on board, as we do every piece of information, and at the moment, believe me, all avenues are being explored.' He sits back and I realise I'm being dismissed. I thought I'd done all I could anyway, so get up to leave.

As Pattison shows me to the door, he says, 'Thank you for coming in so quickly to run through your statement again. It's been helpful for us but please remember what I said before about keeping the details to yourself?' I tell him I haven't forgotten, hold myself back from asking them to go easy on Charlie and leave the room. Barker guides me to the front desk and says goodbye. Like yesterday, he's not said much the whole time, but I suspect that's the point of him. He's doesn't ask the questions; he observes intently with his eager little eyes. No doubt picking up on nuances in behaviour and answers. Or maybe that's my paranoia.

I'm deep in thought as I walk out of the front doors of the station, the murky afternoon already darkening towards night, and I walk along the road and stand at the kerb waiting to cross to where I'd parked my car. As I check for traffic, I'm surprised to see Eric come out of a side road to the right and walk rapidly along the pavement on the other side of the road. Eric is the rather harried husband of Sharon and, as far as I am aware, still commutes each day to London for work, so it is strange to see him around on a weekday. Although maybe he is still on his Christmas break. He glances over, but although I raise my hand in greeting he blanks me, which is odd.

By the time I cross the road he has disappeared round the corner and, putting the incident to the back of my mind, I hurry to my car, keen to get home and not leave afternoon stables entirely to Harry and Pip.

I call Seb from outside the village and ask him to open the gates up if the reporters are still there. He mutters darkly that they are and says he'll do it now.

He is waiting as I return, shuts the gates and is by my side quicker than I can get out of the car. I appreciate his protection as he shepherds me inside, past the enthusiastic attentions of Scout, to where he has a welcome and decent mug of tea waiting, and wants to know how it went. I hear Pattison's words of warning and, not sure how much I should say, I keep it to the bare bones. This satisfies his curiosity, particularly once I tell him they've taken Charlie in for questioning.

'It's always someone close to the family.' A reminder of Pattison saying much the same thing earlier.

'Yes, but not Charlie, he wouldn't hurt a fly,' I insist as I say it's only procedural anyway, him being taken in, but he gives me a knowing look which I choose to ignore as he knows no more than anyone else, and finish my tea quickly so I can change and head for the yard.

I'm relieved once I'm doing some physical work and can shrug off the last couple of hours. Pip is sorting out the ponies in the paddocks when Harry stops by as I finish grooming Candy and am replacing her rugs for the night. He let me be when I first arrived, knowing I needed some time, but now he wants to find out how I got on. He looks worse than earlier; shadows deepen the hollows beneath his eyes.

'It was fine,' I say. 'It was only adding to my statement after all, but I was ridiculously nervous being back in that place.'

'Do they know about Matt yet?'

'Oh yes, although they didn't dwell on it.'

'Well, they wouldn't, would they? Because you were innocent.' I exit the stable and avoid his eye contact.

'They *found me* innocent, Harry. Doesn't mean I was.'

'You are the only person who still thinks you're guilty, Laura.' We have had this conversation repeatedly. He'd never convince me. Never. And if he couldn't, nobody could. Because he'd been part of the tragedy. He'd been there that night, in the car. He and his girlfriend. She didn't hang around for long after and I don't give her much thought, but I do Harry. I often wonder if he has the same images that come to my mind in the dark hours of the night. If I don't block them out with pills, that is. He's told me he doesn't, but then he would say that, wouldn't he? To make me feel better. He's spent years trying to make me feel that.

Six years ago we'd gone for an ordinary night out. A meal in a pub in a village a few miles away. A place we often went. Good food. Friendly atmosphere. The run-up to Christmas. The place was famous for its steaks and that's what we had, with a bottle of red. I joined the others in a glass. We finished eating and went through to the bar. Friends had arrived we'd not seen in months and we caught up, the evening getting away from us as we chatted, and laughed and had fun. Matt leaned on me when we walked out later. None too steady, the icy crunch underfoot in stark contrast to the rosy glow we'd left. Harry laughed as he made a joke about pouring his girl into the back seat. I was worried she'd be sick. Hoped I'd get her home before that happened.

The journey was standard.

Until it wasn't.

The country lane quiet. Headlights in the distance blinked on and off as corners were negotiated, hedges and gateways passed. Then steady. And bright. Full beam on as they hit the straight towards us. I slowed, slowed again, like a rabbit caught in the headlights. I pulled to the left, cowered, and dazzled. The ditch prevented further escape. Matt urged me on, told me to be brave. Told me it would be all right, told me there'd be enough room...

I stayed put.

The car hit us head on. No move made to alter course. No move made to brake. The driver asleep at the wheel. Drunk, it turned out after they completed all the investigations.

The explosion of the moment is what jolts me in the night. The noise of impact, of metal screeching, of shattering glass. Of screams. Dust as airbags deployed. Wet that splattered my face. The violence of the collision forced my car off the road, threw us in the ditch.

Near silence.

Nothing from the other car. Whimpers from ours.

I heard movement behind. Harry asked if everyone was okay. His girl cried. Vomited.

I looked over at Matt. Saw only red.

A jagged scream that's never left my throat.

A branch had come through his window. Nothing to be done.

I held his hand until they cut me from the vehicle. Until it cooled in mine.

If I hadn't had that glass of wine, Matt might still be here. It's as simple as that in my mind and as I can't undo that decision, we'll never know. The fact I'd had the wine hours beforehand and with a meal, to me was irrelevant. The fact I'd passed the breathalyser test was of no consequence. I believed I was guilty of killing my husband then and I still do today. Because my decision-making *may* have been impeded. If it hadn't been, if I had been completely on the ball, I might have saved us... That is the thought that will forever haunt me. So today, as always, I ignore what Harry has to say on the topic as he knows I will. He carries on, 'I actually stopped by to say I have to leave early so I've got as far as I can.'

'Okay no problem, and thank you.' He always asks, like he's in my permanent employ or something, but I owe him for more hours than I can count, so he tells me which horses he's finished so I know where to start.

'Anything exciting?' I ask, wondering if he has a big night out planned. It's unlikely in the circumstances, but you never know.

'Er, no,' and he looks shifty, finds staring at his feet irresistible, 'actually, I, er, I have to go to the police station.'

'Oh!' I'm taken by surprise. He waves it off, but the worry lines between his eyes have deepened in the last couple of days. 'They… don't… suspect you, do they?'

'I'm sure they suspect everyone. But they've invited me in rather than turn up with the handcuffs, so I think I'm all right.' He smiles but sees my concern and puts a hand on my shoulder. 'Don't,' he says, and he gives me that look which tells me not to worry. 'They'll want to talk to everyone who knew the family. You told me that.' I know he's right. It makes perfect sense, and I shake my head to dispel my concern.

'Yes, of course.' I'm relieved. 'You will let me know when you're back, though, won't you?'

'Yes. Stop worrying,' and with a reassuring smile, he ambles off, appearing as relaxed as anything, I'm sure for my benefit.

Once work is done for the day, I make a simple dinner to keep occupied, fretting alternately between Harry, and Charlie, and his poor mother. She must be worried sick. I don't know her well, but I know Sally was widowed when Charlie was about twelve and it's only been the two of them ever since.

She'll be devastated, and I wonder if she has anyone around to support her and how she would feel if I popped in to see how she is.

When I mention this to Seb, though, I can see it makes him uncomfortable and when I push for his thoughts, he reluctantly admits he doesn't think it's a good idea. I'm certain all the media attention has spooked him as he tells me "Now I've done my bit", as he calls it, "perhaps I should back off and let the police handle everything". He thinks that would take me out of the limelight as far as the press are concerned, a fact I hadn't considered but welcomed. I know he's got my best interests at heart, but it doesn't sit easily with me; Sally and Charlie are part of the community I've spent my entire life in. You can't simply turn your back on that. However, I daresay Charlie is back home by now anyway, so maybe I'm making something out of nothing.

I receive a text from Harry shortly after seven saying he's safe and sound in his flat so I can stop fretting. We have a brief exchange as I'm keen to know what they asked, but he says it was pretty general. What was his relationship with the family? Could he account for his movements on the night of the thirtieth of December? Straightforward stuff, he added, as he thought. He got the impression they would do the same with anyone who knew the family. As I end the text conversation with him, I consider if that were the case, they were going to be incredibly busy. Seb interrupts my thoughts.

'Who are you texting?'

'Harry. He's back home.' I'd told Seb over dinner about him going into the station, so briefly updated him on what they wanted. 'He says it looks like they will speak to everyone who knew the family.' I glance over at him. 'So expect a call.'

75

'Me? I barely knew them.'

'You've been living here for over two years, Seb. You've spent plenty of time with them.'

'Two years, is it? Already! Doesn't time fly when you're having fun?'

I smile over at him, but my mind is full of only one thing. It appears the police have settled on the date of death for the Jackson family.

8: Sharon Spouts Her Poison.

There are a few reporters back outside the house in the morning. I'm not sure what they're hoping to gain, as it must be pretty clear by now that no one here is going to talk to them. I've learned my lesson. Say one word and they will print stuff out of context and cause so much harm it's simply not worth trying to tell them anything. I try to explain this to Seb when he suggests I tell them what I know, as that will give them what they want and they'll go away, but he doesn't get it because he wasn't around when Matt died. Although of course that was different, as I was being vilified in the press back then. I haven't looked at the papers this time because I know they will have dredged up my past. I know this because of the way Seb has been looking at me. If he didn't know all the grubby details about the part I played in Matt's death before, he does now. I suspect this was behind his idea for me to speak to them. They'd have something new to feast on. But I know it doesn't work like that.

Anyway, this morning I have to get a few bits and pieces in to replenish the cupboards. Not needing enough to warrant a trip to a supermarket in town, I decide to go to the village shop. In general I'd walk, but I'm unlikely to shake off the questions that way, so I get in the car and, as Seb is busy in his office, ask Harry to open the front gates for me.

As soon as I enter the shop, I know it's a mistake.

I scoot in, nip up the first aisle while Sharon's busy with a customer, but I can hear her at the till telling all who pass her way about the news of Charlie being arrested. She has one of those voices that carry. Once I get over the shock that Charlie has apparently been kept overnight, I become incensed by her spreading such lies. Snatching what I need from the shelves, I call out, 'He's not been arrested, Sharon, he's helping the police with their enquiries, like many other men around here are doing.' It's worrying though to discover that, unlike Harry, he hasn't been allowed back home.

'That's as good as, in my opinion,' she raises her voice in response, shouting over the shelving. 'You mark my words, he's a bad lot.'

'Don't be ridiculous!' I'll be lucky if I haven't broken the eggs I throw in my basket. 'You've known Charlie since he was born. You know, as well as I do, he's not capable of this.' I join the back of the short queue that probably wouldn't be there at all if Sharon didn't spend quite so much of her time gossiping. She lowers her voice, as though to share a confidence with the woman she's serving, but not enough so we can't all hear, as she expounds her ignorance further.

'There's no smoke without fire. That's what I always say and I can tell you something for nothing. I feel safer in my bed knowing he's no longer prowling the streets.' Sharon's caustic tone buoys my anger. How can she be so callous about one of our own? Like me, she is part of this community and it shocks me how immediately she's assumed his guilt, completely dismissing the possibility of innocence.

Her words will do nothing to calm people's fears in the village, either. What with the murders naturally being the focus of everyone's mind and dominating every discussion, together with the police making house-to-house enquiries, there is undoubtedly an increased level of anxiety and agitation, bordering on hysteria in some places.

The person in front of me is hunched over, as though trying to disappear into the overcoat that nearly reaches to the ground, a dark hat pulled low on her brow. I hear a sob as her basket drops to the ground and she mutters, 'Excuse me, excuse me,' as she edges her way past those in front of her before making a dash for the exit, and as she turns left out of the door I glimpse her profile.

Sally.

Poor woman. My heart sinks.

'Look what your venom has done, Sharon,' I say as I pick up Sally's basket. 'You should be ashamed of yourself.' Her cheeks colour, but she still can't help herself.

'I'm only speaking the truth.'

'No, you're not, and if you have nothing nice to say, I suggest you say nothing at all.'

She takes a deep breath of disapproval through pinched nostrils and now that it's my turn to be served, she processes both my basket and Sally's as if she has an unpleasant smell under her nose. I continue to come in here for the convenience but I know there are others who won't set foot in the place. She has no idea of the damage she does or the hurt she causes.

We complete the transaction without exchanging another word. I walk out, vowing to never darken this doorway again. However, I know the moment I've run out of milk I will be back because there's no reasonable alternative, and that only serves to irritate the hell out of me.

I get in the car and continue on in the same direction up Main Road. Spotting Sally a few hundred metres away. I pull alongside and lower the window.

'Would you like a lift? She looks over, her expression reminding me of a timid rabbit about to cry, and nods without speaking as she reaches for the door handle. She exhales once she's in and clutches her bag on her lap with a vice-like grip. I say nothing as we make the short journey to her home.

She lives in a cul-de-sac on the small estate at the end of the village and as I turn into it, she cries out in alarm. The television crew are there, together with many I recognise from the street outside The Stables yesterday. They've found their next doorstep to haunt.

'Don't worry,' I say, trying to sound braver than I feel. 'I'll help get you into the house. But we're going to have to move through them quickly, understand?' I glance across at Sally and she nods in response. 'Okay, have your key ready.' She rummages in her bag and draws it out as I drive towards the small crowd and pull over to the kerb. All eyes turn towards us. I ask Sally to stay where she is. Lifting her bag of groceries from the back seat behind me, I get out and go round to the passenger side. I open the door and, shielding her from the reporters, encourage her to get out. I then take her arm to keep close and we march with intent towards the crowd, there being no other way to reach her front door. Sally is shorter than me and has to scuttle along to keep up, but momentum is needed. The questions start, phones or furry mics held in our direction and tracking our progress, but we don't hesitate, not for a single second. Nor do we make eye contact. 'No comment,' I say as, refusing to be intimidated, we battle our way through, Sally's front door our goal. We reach it, Sally's key finds its home and we are inside, relieved to be in the relative peace. I breathe deeply, not having expelled my held breath since exiting the car. I draw the curtains in the front room so no one can see in, then turn my attention to Sally. She's badly shaken. Removing her hat and coat, I guide her to the sofa and make her sit. I go to fill the kettle, flicking it on, and put her groceries away while it comes to the boil. We haven't said a word since we got inside and I'm not sure where to start. I end up taking two mugs of strong tea back into the front room, place hers on the small table at her side and, sitting in the chair that's at right angles to hers, hold mine in my lap.

'I've put sugar in it,' I say, indicating towards her drink. 'It'll help with the shock, so I'm told.' She smiles weakly in my direction. 'Have you heard anything yet?' She shakes her head. 'Well, they have to either charge or release him within twenty-four hours, so he could be home soon.' I try to be reassuring and don't add that I also know they can extend that period to thirty-six or even ninety-six hours with a serious crime, such as murder.

'How do you kn—' and she bites off her words, looking away in embarrassment when she remembers why I would know about the process.

'Don't worry,' I brush away her awkwardness, 'they found me innocent and they will Charlie, too.' She smiles again, probably from relief that I'm not offended. She looks exhausted, her pale face like putty, dark bags under her eyes, and I wonder if she slept at all last night. 'Can I ask? Does he have a solicitor with him?' Her eyes widen in alarm.

'I don't know? Does he need one?'

'He should have one and they will have offered him a duty solicitor,' I hope he had the sense to take up the offer. 'Tell you what, would you like me to call my solicitor? See if he can help?' She agrees gratefully and I see tears well up in her eyes as I reach for my phone. It's a Saturday but Steve always had liked the quiet of the office at the weekend to catch up on some work and I thought little would have changed.

I hear the cautious note of surprise in his voice as he answers, but once I assure him I'm not in any trouble, we have a swift catch-up and I explain the problem. He, as I knew he would, says he'll go to the station, find out what's going on and take over supporting Charlie if I want him to. I say I do and end the call. If nothing else, at least we now have a contact who will tell us what's going on.

I try to comfort Sally. 'There we go. He'll give Charlie some help.'

'Thank you and thank you for the groceries, too. I'll give you the money.' She looks round for her bag.

'Don't worry about it. You have enough on your plate.' I sip my tea. It's nearly cool enough. 'Have you got any family nearby who could come over?'

She shakes her head. 'No, I've got a sister up in Northumberland. That's where we were over New Year, but I don't want to bother her with this. Not yet, anyway.' She thinks for a moment. 'I have some friends locally. I'm sure they'll help.' Then a doubtful look creeps over her face as though she's uncertain of their loyalty under these circumstances. I wonder what her friends might make of the situation.

'Remember that not everyone is like Sharon, Sally. In fact, fortunately, most people aren't.' I try to reassure her. 'Do you want me to stay until someone else can come over?'

'No, you're all right. I'll call them later.'

'Okay, are you able to stay put for the time being? It's probably best if you don't go out.'

'I don't have to go into work until Tuesday and hopefully he'll be home and it'll all be over long before then.' I agree with her as I finish my tea and take the mugs out to the kitchen. It's time I was on my way as I need to get back to work. 'Thanks for your help, Laura, it's much appreciated,' she says as I re-enter the room.

'You're welcome. Are you sure you're going to be all right? Because I should get back to the yard. You've got my number, haven't you? Call me if you need anything.' She says she has and she will, and as she looks brighter now I feel happier to leave.

'I hope he's home soon, Sally.'

'I hope so too,' she replies as I see myself out, steeling myself to battle through the throng again.

I'd left my phone in the car while with Sally, and when I check it I find a message from Seb telling me the police have asked him into the station for questioning. Fortunately he doesn't ask where I am, presumably preoccupied with the request from the police. He says he's going straight away to get it over with and he'll see me later. I'm less worried for him than I would have been if Harry hadn't already been through the same so I return to The Stables, the entrance of which is now clear of journalists, receive a joyous reception from Scout when I let her out and we walk over to the yard together.

Seb is back only a couple of hours later when I'm busy in the stables. Unusually, he comes to find me in the yard. I'm sorting Nebula, having exercised her in the menage after her owner rang to say she couldn't make it because of a clash in her diary. Well, it is a tad bitter out today.

I sense someone behind me and turn to find Seb there, leaning on the half door.

'You're back,' I say with a smile. 'Did it go okay?'

'Standard questions, like you said. I thought I'd see you before I went, though. Why were you so long this morning?'

'There was a bit of an issue in the shop. Sharon was being particularly nasty about Charlie, and Sally was actually there, in the queue. It was horrible. Anyway, Sally walked out, and I went after her.'

'Of course you did.'

'She needed help, Seb. Sharon was completely out of line.'

'I understand, Laura,' he smiles at me, 'I shouldn't have expected you to be anything other than yourself. Sorry if I wasn't supportive before.' He opens the door enough to step inside.

'Apology accepted.' I grin at him as I tighten the surcingle on Nebula's rug. 'I'm sorry too. I shouldn't assume you understand that because Sally lives in the village I've spent my life in, I feel it makes it my duty to help.' Turning towards him, he puts his arms around me, draws me close.

'I don't understand you mean, because I'm the outsider.' I hate it when he does that. It's not what I meant, but it stands to reason I have a greater affinity to the place than he does. Because of my birth and business, I know most people here. I've known many all my life.

'Outsider or not, I'm pleased I helped her out, as the reporters were all over her doorstep when we got there.' I link my hands round the back of his neck, which I caress with my thumb.

'So now they're going to have even more photos of you being mixed up in this case.' I hadn't thought about that, but what difference does it make, anyway? Whether or not he likes it, I am mixed up in it. I shrug, not knowing how to respond. 'I told you, you've done your bit.' He leans in for a kiss, which I swerve.

'You told me, did you?' He knows I like nothing less than being told to do something. However, this is accelerating into a row and I don't want that, not in the current circumstances. I release him and lift a placating hand. 'Look, let's leave it there, shall we? I can't change anything now, anyway. I am sorry I wasn't here to see you off earlier. Perhaps you can tell me all about it over dinner?'

Somewhat mollified, he says, 'Of course, I'm sorry too. I'll organise something to eat.' His hands loosen on my waist and he leaves the stable.

'We could also finish what we started here,' I say, wanting to get past this sticky moment as soon as possible.

His smile relaxes his face. 'I'll look forward to that.'

He's stirring a pan when I walk in. Without a word, he moves it off the heat, puts the lid on, and takes my hand to lead me upstairs. His mind has not moved on far from our last words. Which is fine, as long as he doesn't mind the pre-shower me.

Our bedroom is in darkness, the only light through the window from street lamps. He turns until he's behind me and slides the band off my ponytail. My hair cascades around my shoulders and I hear his intake of breath. He moves my curls to one side and my lips part as his graze my neck, hot breath igniting a path to my core. Slipping his hands in under my sweatshirt, he pulls my tee shirt out of my jodhpurs, then removes the lot over my head. He unclips my bra and, as it falls to the floor, he holds me close, caresses my breasts, my nipples tightening. I push back into him, keen to feel his desire as he presses himself against my bottom. I reach to undo his trousers but he pushes my hands away, concentrates on undoing mine instead. His fingers trail across my stomach, skim my hips, his tongue flickers against my neck. A sensation that's hard to ignore. I hook my thumbs into the waistband of my jodhpurs and push them down, bending over as I do so. His breath

85

deepens as he holds me around the waist, grinds against me. I stand and turn towards him. We kiss, lips soft, tongues lithe, sensuous, as I undo buttons, open his shirt and move closer, skin to skin. I continue downwards, undo the button, the zip, then hear him groan as I reach inside. Sometimes we take our time, warm up, linger over foreplay. This is not one of those occasions. I push him to sit on the bed, climb astride and take him inside in one movement. My fingers thread through his hair, then tighten and I tip his head back. We kiss, lips hard. I drive down to possess every inch of him, then move slowly, tilting my hips as sensation builds, then faster, driving against him as we each strive for satisfaction. My release explodes within; waves of pleasure ripple out from my core as he cries out, then holds me tight as aftershocks rock my body.

We still. Stay curled around each other.

'I think we both needed that,' he says, as foreheads together, our breaths calm.

'Uh huh,' I murmur.

Later, when I've showered and am in my pyjamas, he serves up dinner and we talk as we eat. I persuade him to tell me everything that happened at the police station. It's an unsettling thing to go through, so I understand the need for him to share and I make appropriate noises to encourage him. Like Harry, they had asked him how he knew the family and where he was on the night of the thirtieth of December. That one was easy, of course, because he was with me.

9: Suspects?

Every day the Jacksons are my first thought on waking, my last before my sleeping pill overwhelms me each night, and between those times, my mind is never far from them. The feeling of loss and grief tinged with disbelief that they are gone. If I get distracted, for even the shortest time, and question that fact, I'm jolted back into reality with the horrible truth that, yes, this has actually happened.

Tears are never far away. They spill over at the slightest trigger, the myriad of memories that flood my mind, the carnage I witnessed. Consequently, my head pounds with the constant pressure.

Then there's the paralysis that threatens to grind my world to a halt. I feel it creeping over me. The difficulty rising each morning. The ability to sit and stare at nothing, and finding myself standing with some piece of equipment in hand and no recollection of whether I've already used it or am about to.

However, life cannot simply stop and we have to get on with business as usual in the yard and Sunday is a busy day for lessons. I always help Pip get the ponies ready. I'm especially pleased to do so right now, anything to occupy me most welcome.

Pip came to me a couple of years ago and presented me with a proposition to expand my business by offering riding lessons. I'm not qualified to deliver them but she was newly so, and, as I wanted to support someone who was keen to work with horses but hadn't had the advantages I had, I said yes. The livery side of the business is mine. Pip keeps Pegasus with me in exchange for a certain number of hours of work a month. We own all the riding school ponies jointly and Pip earns her money teaching, which is what she loves. I get a percentage and we split any expenses. It's a system that's worked for a while now and to the satisfaction of us both.

The ponies live outside, unless the weather is terrible, but on days when Pip has lessons they come into the yard, and we've added a sturdy shelter running along the side of the hay barn. This comprises a row of small stables, or stalls might be a more accurate description, although they have doors to them. They're too small to house a pony in permanently but perfectly adequate on a temporary, or overnight, basis. The ponies can turn around in them, get groomed, tacked up and left to nibble at a hay net if they are in there for any length of time. It helps to keep them dry and comfortable on days when they might be in and out for different lessons.

We have around thirty ponies now. The ones that are needed for today have spent the night either in this row, or loose in the indoor school, so they are dry and clean before they start work. While Pip is already taking the first class, I tack up Honey, a pretty palomino, as a couple of the youngsters that help us out are doing the same to Biggles and Charm in readiness for the next busier lesson.

Harry always likes a lie-in on Sundays as he often works at the pub Saturday night. It is also most likely to be the day when we don't see him at all as he spends it on his artistic pursuits. He says he likes the creative feel of a Sunday and it helps that he has no other work to interrupt his flow. But not today. He arrives mid-morning looking tired and hungover. He has no spare flesh on him anyway and we've often teased him about having cheekbones a model would envy, along with thick lashes that Pip says are wasted on a boy. But today his face is drawn, as if he's lost weight. The hollows beneath his eyes dark.

'Not sculpting today?' I say, concerned at the state of him.

'No,' he replies, then smiles, distracted as he gazes across the yard, 'the creative muse is not co-operating. I thought I'd come and keep busy instead.' I can empathise with him on that need, but there is something about him that worries me. We are all struggling, but he's taking it hardest and again I wonder about the depth of his relationship with Jenny.

I try to keep an eye on him as we crack on with the morning's work. There are a lot more people around the yard at the weekend: livery owners, the older kids that help, along with a lot of children that come for lessons, and their parents. Naturally, there is one principal topic of conversation and although I try to keep myself to myself, I still face several people who want to show their concern. Touching and lovely of them, but I'd prefer it if people weren't so kind. It would be easier to handle.

It is also clear how fast news spreads. We heard several times over the course of the day of other men who have been taken in for questioning by the police. Eric, from the shop, and goodness only knows what Sharon will make of that. I imagine her bristling when asked about it by customers. How her tune would change when it was her own husband in for questioning. The vitriol she spewed about Charlie would be gone and she'd be all, 'Oh, he's doing his duty so the police can eliminate him from their enquiries.' The landlord of the pub, Mike, was another, along with several of the regulars, and Ned, the local handyman. Apparently, all the staff on the Melton Estate had volunteered to go to the police station and assist the police in any way they could. How much of this was true and how much

89

fabricated was hard to tell, but the crucial fact, sadly not invented, was that they had still not released Charlie. I send Sally a couple of supportive texts and follow up with a quick call. She thanks me again for enlisting Steve's services and tells me he has been keeping her up to date with progress. Not that there is much. The police were granted extra time to question Charlie, and it worries me they clearly had enough evidence to do that.

Several of the regulars.

I assume that includes Gary Sykes. He is someone I steer well clear of as he behaved completely inappropriately after Matt died. Still gives me the shivers. He's a quiet bloke. Single. In fact, I don't remember him ever having a girlfriend. Works on a local farm and shoot. He appeared in the yard within a couple of days of the accident, offering help, which was kind of him. Many people were equally thoughtful. We were due a delivery of straw, and he took charge of the unloading. Did the same with a feed delivery a couple of days later. He'd spot odd jobs around the yard and arrive with his toolbox. Muck in with everyone else in getting the work done when I was barely functioning. All helpful stuff.

Then, I couldn't get rid of him.

He'd call round before and after work to see if I needed anything. He'd contact me every time he was going to any type of retailer to see if I wanted any shopping doing.

I admit I was so numb with grief I didn't see what was happening.

But one night I drew my curtains when I went to bed, and saw his car parked out on the road, him inside.

That, I noticed.

The day after Matt's funeral, he asked me out. *The day after*. I'm not sure I've ever been more shocked. I thought I'd misheard. When he repeated himself, he did not mishear the berating that followed. Neither did most of the village, of that I'm sure. My grief boiling over into a fury of such savagery, I questioned my sanity afterwards.

He hasn't so much as met my eye since.

Gary must be high on the suspect list. How could he not be?

I am also interested and intrigued by the fact that Eric is being questioned. After seeing him that day outside the police station, it had occurred to me that perhaps he was on his way to talk to them. Was this a second conversation? In which case, perhaps he was a person of interest. That would certainly ruffle Sharon's feathers.

I know little about him, but in my mind, Eric is decidedly odd. For one thing he married Sharon, and while I can forgive someone being blinded by love into taking a swift trip up the aisle, I find it truly astonishing that having got to know her over many years he chooses to remain married to her. He also works away from home, which gives him considerable freedom. Who knows what goes on during those long work days, and he must cherish his time away, as he shows no interest in coming to work alongside Sharon in the shop. She makes no secret about who wears the trousers in that relationship and she constantly undermines him. More than a few eyes have rolled when she's been less than discreet about their sex life, or more precisely, their lack of one.

It makes you wonder, doesn't it? Are they in separate bedrooms? If so, that would give him ample opportunity to sneak away in the night. Because, if a man isn't getting it at home, what lengths might he go to in order to get it elsewhere?

I go into the house and start on the rolls. It has become a tradition that I provide Sunday lunch for anyone working at the yard, which involves me making around thirty bacon rolls. It's quite a task and although I don't feel like it, I do it anyway because, well, because that's what we do around here. I leave a couple behind for Seb, who I can hear talking on his phone in his office, and load up a tray with the rest wrapped in foil, sachets of red and brown sauce on the side, and carry it out to the yard in time for the break from lessons. Lunch happens in the tack room as built-in wooden storage lockers line the walls and provide seating.

The atmosphere is unnaturally subdued, and at first everyone consumes the rolls in silence. Harry boils the kettle over by the sink and makes mugs of steaming tea for all. The kids take their food and flop onto the boxes to eat. They are always ravenous, which is why I make so many.

'Did everything go smoothly in the lessons this morning?' I ask Pip, which is mistimed as she's just taken a bite of her roll. She rocks her head back and forth as she tries to clear her mouth and one youngster, a red-headed girl about twelve called Gemma, giggles.

'Rusty sat down halfway through the lesson.'

'Ahh,' I say, feeling a twist in my stomach, 'And the rider?' Lessons make me anxious, it's why I never teach.

'She stayed on. He was careful, of course.'

'I'm sure he was.' Rusty is a rascal. At around thirty years of age, he is the oldest of our ponies and probably the most mischievous. If he feels he doesn't want to take part in the lesson, he will sit, most carefully, and without tipping the rider off. The helper has to clip on a lead rein, encourage him back up and the lesson will continue, no harm done.

'Anything else?' I direct my question back at Pip, who can speak this time.

'Beau dumped Stuart on the floor again.'

'And yet he always asks to ride her.'

'I know, I don't get it either,' she shakes her head. 'I'll put him on something safer next time, I think. Probably Goldie.'

'Good idea.' Beau is a fluffy cremello, which is unusual in itself, but he has an unnerving habit of depositing on the floor those who do not sit up properly. Fortunately the surface of the indoor school is soft, so we rarely have injuries, and many pupils who stay the course have learned to have excellent seats because of Beau's rather unusual teaching methods.

Goldie, on the other hand, is a super palomino who is as safe as houses and excellent for all children to begin on. His winter coat is the colour of pale fudge, but come the summer it sheds to reveal the sleekest coat of the richest butterscotch.

Once the tales of the morning have been told, it relaxes us all and a bit of chat ensues. Not a lot, but enough to make it more comfortable for the kids. Once everyone has eaten their fill, they drift back out to the yard to get ready for the afternoon lessons because the first pupils are already arriving. I see there is one roll left. I offer it to Harry, who has not said a word all lunchtime when normally he is the life and soul of the place. He is still sitting morosely in one corner and takes the roll reluctantly, and then only because I practically force it on him. I sit next to him. He has gradually disappeared into himself over the last few days, and I don't like it.

'Do you want to talk?'

'There's not much to say.' He looks miserable and I think it will do him good to have someone to chat with. It's not like he has anyone at home to unload on.

'Look, I know things are dark and it's early days, but you're taking this particularly badly. Is there anything I can do to help?' He shakes his head. 'Was it awful at the police station? Are you concerned about that?'

He looks at me as if he's tussling with whether or not to say anything, then leans forward and with his elbows on his knees, holds his head in his hands. 'I don't want you to think badly of me.'

'I never could.' I place my hand on his shoulder and give it a squeeze, to reassure him, but we're interrupted by Gemma bounding into the tack room to get one of the pony's saddles. Harry, who had leaned in to me and tilted his face as if about to speak, sits back up, then stands, muttering that he has to get on.

It's frustrating, then made more so as I have no further chance to speak to him because he finishes shortly thereafter and goes home. I send him a text later offering a non-judgemental ear but get no response.

That evening, I can't help but dwell on what he said. Exactly what is it he's done that makes him feel I'll think badly of him?

10: The Wrong Man?

There's no milk left for breakfast the next morning. Annoyed I have to enter the shop again, I rush up Main Street after doing the early feeds in the yard, and enter the shop at the perfect moment to hear occasional shop assistant, Dora Smith, ask, 'And they've kept him in all night?' She's speaking to Sharon, who glances over, then quickly drops her eyes from mine. She's flushed, which intrigues me. I walk swiftly to the refrigerated unit to get the milk. Unfortunately for Sharon, this doesn't take me out of earshot and despite her dropping her voice, I can still hear her reply.

'That means nothing.' She sounds like she's speaking through gritted teeth.

'It's not a good sign though, is it?' Dora leans closer towards Sharon. 'I mean, other than Charlie, I haven't heard that the police have questioned anyone for that long.'

It piques my interest who they're talking about and while I've a good idea, I don't have the time to hang around and work it out, so I jump right in. 'Who's been kept in all night?' Sharon inhales sharply and can't bear to look at me. Dora is not so reticent.

'Eric.' My heart gives a tiny leap of joy. This is too good. I mean, obviously it's not great for Eric, but even so, a priceless moment such as this can't be ignored.

'Noooo…' I put way too much emphasis on one paltry word, and I hear Sharon's tut before she snaps back at me.

'It wasn't him.'

'Of course it wasn't.' I tilt my head in that understanding way people do. 'But you know what they say, Sharon? There's no smoke without fire.'

'I'm telling you, it wasn't him.' The colour is high in her cheeks.

'I wonder if people in the village slept better last night knowing he wasn't prowling the streets.' There's a certain satisfaction in repeating her words back to her and as my work here is done, I place my coins on the counter, pick up my milk and walk out. As I do so, I pass Eric on his way in. He looks remarkably chipper, considering the night he's had.

'Hope you're all right,' I say as we pass, determined to play nice. Innocent until proven guilty, and all that.

'Thank you.' He gives me a smile tinged with what looks like relief and while part of me wants to hang around to see what sort of reception he receives, the better part of me leaves them to it.

As I head back to the stables, I get a notification on the village email that there is to be a vigil outside Number 9 this evening. It's one week on from the deaths, it bleakly reminds me.

Pattison and Barker arrive at The Stables shortly after ten. It is Monday. The pupils have gone back to school, so the yard is quieter than it has been for a while. Routinely Harry and I would exercise out together, but this morning he'd tacked up his favourite ride Wooster, said he needed some space and gone out. That was two hours ago.

We usually exercise each horse for an hour to an hour and a half, often having to lead another one each time in order to cover them all, and Pip had helped by coming out with me for the first ride. I sent a text to Harry to check he was all right when we returned, and there was no sign of him. He had answered with a monosyllabic yes, but he still hadn't come back. Pip and I are in the middle of organising our next ride out when the police appear.

I am leading Sahara out of her stable and already have Nebula ready, and when the two officers walk straight into the yard, my stomach drops at the sight of them.

I try to appear calm and as I walk towards the detectives, leading both horses, say, 'Morning, can I help you?' Sahara is part Arabian and gets terribly fidgety in her stable if I don't take her out each morning, so she's keen to be off, mouthing her bit as she tosses her head.

'Is Harry O'Connor here?' Pattison sets his face, giving nothing away.

'No, well, yes, at least he will be,' is my confused response. Pattison's eyebrow rises. I explain further, 'He's out at the moment, on Wooster. He'll be back, if you want to wait.'

'Do you know how long he'll be?'

'No. We mostly only ride out for an hour.' And I stop talking as I realise what I've said.

'And when did he leave?' I check my watch for no reason other than to stall.

'About eight.' Now I've already opened my big mouth, there's no point in lying. Barker glances at his phone.

'So, nearly two and a half hours ago?'

'He said he wanted some space.' I hear the hooves of Pip's two horses, Flame and Candy, as they join us in the centre of the yard and as they come to a standstill behind us, I hear more hooves at a distance. Relief floods through me. 'That'll be him now.' Pattison's expression relaxes marginally as both he and

Barker turn to look towards the entrance gate, but do nothing to disguise their presence. Pip and I stay put.

'What do you want with him?' I ask, not expecting an answer, so I'm surprised when Barker says,

'Just a chat.'

The main gates to the property are permanently open again now the danger of marauding reporters is over. At that moment Harry turns Wooster in through them and approaches the yard gates. These are always kept shut in case any horse gets loose. As is usual, Harry comes to a halt, dismounts and opens the gate to allow him and the horse through. He closes it behind him and turns to face us all.

'Hope you haven't been waiting long.' He doesn't appear to be in anyway surprised to see the police there, not reacting in the slightest when he first turned in through the gate even though he must have spotted them, and he appears resigned when Pattison approaches.

'Harry O'Connor, I'd like you to come with us. We have a few more questions.'

'Do I have a choice?'

'I don't want to arrest you, Harry, but I will do so if necessary.' I hear Pip's gasp behind me.

'No!' My reaction causes Harry to look at me. He tries a rueful smile, shakes his head. Barker holds out a pair of handcuffs. 'You don't need those.' I can't bear to see Harry marched away in them, like some... and I have to steel myself, like some criminal.

'She's right,' Harry says, 'I'll come quietly. It's only a few more questions, after all.' He removes his hat and holds that and Wooster's reins out to me. 'Sorry to leave you with that handful.'

'It doesn't matter,' I say, as Barker turns Harry around, places a hand on his shoulder and moves him back towards the gate which Pattison is opening. They appear unmoved and not in the mood for pleas, but I can't help myself.

'I know you didn't do it, Harry,' I call out, sure the police will ignore whatever I say. So far in their eyes, I have thought no one they suspect can be guilty. I watch, helpless, as they take Harry to the police car and direct him into the rear seat. As the door closes, he turns to look back at me through the window, but I can't read his expression. *Believe in me? I'm innocent?* I'm not sure. But I'm reminded of the conversation we didn't quite have yesterday and the fact I knew he wanted to tell me something.

I stare after the police car as it drives away, and notice Seb standing outside our back door, watching the action unfold. He walks over and leans on the yard gate.

'What's going on?'

'They've taken Harry back in for more questioning.'

'Have they now?' He looks after the car, a thoughtful expression on his face. 'I wouldn't have thought he had it in him.'

'Of course he doesn't have it in him,' I snap. His eyes widen. Realising I now have far too many horses on my hands, I follow it up with, 'Come here and hold these,' and I gesticulate to the reins in my hands. He complies without question, sensing my tone as he hurries to open the gate and I leave him with fidgety Sahara who won't stand still and the only slightly less twitchy Nebula. I edge round them with Wooster, and pass the two Pip is holding. Pip asks if I want her to put him away, but I brush off her offer. I need a moment and as soon as I'm out of sight of the others, I rub tears from my eyes with the heel of my hand.

I sniff and blow out a deep breath as I lead Wooster into his box, then shake myself, refusing to allow any further tears to fall as I quickly take his tack off. Fortunately he's dry, so I fling his rugs on, pin them in place with a surcingle and check he has water and a hay net to occupy him before I leave. I put his tack away and take another deep breath. I'd like nothing more than to cancel the ride out, put the horses back in their boxes and dwell on my own problems instead, but that's the thing with animals, it's unfair on them to not do what they need you to do.

I feel, however, that this new situation with Harry has weighed me down as though a heavy cloak has landed on my shoulders, and it's harder to walk as I make my way back to the waiting horses. I give Pip a pat on the back in passing as I was too brusque with her before and I relieve a tense Seb, who's grimacing while trying to hold each horse at arm's length, with a muttered thank you. Without saying a word, Seb turns to open the gate for us and we go on through. There's a mounting block between these gates and the ones out onto the road and in this yard it's the preferred method of getting on. Once I'm onboard Sahara, I check to see if Seb has closed up behind us, which he has and he responds to my goodbye with a raised arm retreating to the house without breaking stride, no doubt delighted to return to his horse-free world.

Pip and I get ourselves organised and head out onto the road. Sahara is a pain and jogs sideways buzzing with pent-up energy, which makes leading Nebula no easier, so I use my leg to encourage her to straighten up; fortunately there's little traffic around, and as soon as is practicable I push into a trot, keen to drive her forward. Pip will be having an equally challenging ride on Flame, so it's best we get some forward motion going. I'm eager to talk to her but as she's behind me it's difficult to communicate, particularly regarding anything sensitive, so I lead us towards the bridleway that encircles the Melton estate, at which point we can ride four abreast. Slowing to a walk, Sahara's more settled now after the initial release of steam. I look over at Pip. 'What are you thinking?'

She shrugs. 'Other than the fact they've got the wrong man. I'm not sure.' I'm glad she feels the same as I do.

'Do you think this means Charlie is out?'

She shakes her head. 'I don't know. Maybe.' But she sounds doubtful.

'I would have thought Sally would have let me know if he was.' I ponder this for a moment and contemplate calling her, reaching into my pocket for my phone, but then think out loud. 'Actually, I don't want to contact her. It might give her false hope, and that's not fair.'

'That's probably wise.' Pip adjusts her reins.

'So, why do you think they've come for Harry? What's changed?'

'DNA evidence? Maybe the results are back.'

'Of course. But that can't be good. Why would that connect Harry to the crime?' Again I'm wondering out loud but there is no response from Pip and I turn to look at her. She's adjusting her reins again, releases a hand to stroke Flame's neck, and looks to be in no hurry to speak to me. 'Pip?' She reluctantly meets my gaze and I can see she's not keen to talk. 'What do you know? Come on, spit it out.'

'I think Harry might have had some sort of closer relationship with Jenny than we were aware of.'

'That had crossed my mind, but it can't be right because she was going out with Charlie. We all knew that.' Pip makes some sort of noncommittal noise. 'What's that meant to mean?'

101

She turns. 'I don't want to say, I know how close you were to them all.'

'Tell me. I need to know what's going on.' She looks uncomfortable.

'It's only that I don't think Jenny was a one-man-at-a-time sort of woman.'

'Oh,' I hesitate as this information sinks in, feeling a little foolish, old-fashioned and naïve. 'You mean she's been seeing Harry and Charlie?'

Pip shrugs again.

'Possibly. I have no proof, but I've seen how Jenny behaved down the pub and she flirted with a lot of men. It wouldn't surprise me, that's all.' She glances over, grimaces. 'Sorry.'

'No, no, that's all right. I wasn't aware she was like that.' I didn't see her out socialising, so I wasn't familiar with that side of her. What I saw was the eight-year-old Jenny laughing as she and Judy covered John with sand one day at the beach. I realise my experience of the family has coloured my view and I still saw her as she had been. Kids grow up, and change.

'It still doesn't mean Harry did it.'

'No, of course not,' It's good to hear Pip sound as adamant on that fact as I feel, and positive as she continues. 'He'll be back in a couple of hours.' I'm sure she's right, but wonder if I can do anything to help. Of course, it comes to me. Steve. I can get Steve to go in and support him. I pull my phone from my pocket and call him.

'I can't discuss the case with you,' is Steve's answer to my ring.

'I know, but I have another problem.' I explain what's happened to Harry and Steve says he'll send someone. He can't go himself he tells me, that would be unethical as he is already representing Charlie (who is still in custody, the police having applied for further extra time to question him) but he'll make sure Harry has a lawyer present when he's interviewed.

'My bet is he'll be home for afternoon stables,' Pip says with a reassuring smile.

'I hope so,' I say, less confident than she is. 'Meanwhile, we'd better get on. Shall we trot?' and I push Sahara, who needs little encouragement, forward.

Pip would have lost the bet had I taken it, as Harry didn't get back until long after dark. Pip and I are about finished in the yard. She'd done the ponies while I got started on the boxes, then she joined me. All are now clean, with the horses rugged for the night and content with full water buckets, hay nets and last feeds. We check over each door as we make our way towards the gate and then, there he is, Harry, walking into the yard. Pip leaps at him with a full-on hug that nearly takes him off his feet, but I am pleased to hear his chuckle as he wraps his arms around her in return. I'd often considered them to be like brother and sister, but with being so off in my knowledge of the grown-up version of Jenny, I now find myself second guessing this and wondering if there is something between them, too.

'Have you heard about the vigil?' she says, as she releases him.

'No, when is it?'

'Tonight. Eight.' I can see Pip is keen to get off for her dinner, her mum hates her to be late.

'I'll be there.' We say our goodbyes and then we are alone. There's an awkwardness between us that's unusual. He lifts his chin toward the stables and says he wants to check in on the horses. We wander up the yard together slowly, looking over the half door of each box as we go round.

'Thanks for sending Marny,' he says. I'm puzzled. I don't know any Marny, but then it comes to me. Steve.

'You're welcome. I called Steve. He said he'd sort out someone for you. Was she helpful?'

'Yes,' he says, 'it helps to have someone there with you.' There's a pause as he strokes Wooster's nose, but I can't wait any longer. I have to ask.

'Why didn't you tell me about you and Jenny?'

'I tried to, yesterday,' he says, and indicates towards the tack room. I remember. That lost moment.

'But before then. I didn't know you were seeing her.' None of my business of course, but I thought Harry and I were closer than that. I didn't think we kept secrets.

'I wasn't properly seeing her. Not like you're thinking, going out an' that. She had Charlie for the boyfriend stuff.'

'So, what were you?'

'We weren't anything. We had sex, that's all. That's why we kept it to ourselves.' For the first time, I feel old: I can't understand that kind of casual... I was going to call it a relationship, but it's not even that, it's a thing, a casual thing. I'd never done one of those.

I shake my head. 'Sorry, Harry, I shouldn't have asked. It's none of my business what you do, or with whom.' I am happy to leave it there, but he wants to talk.

'I didn't make a big thing of it because of the age difference. I thought people might not be cool with us, you know,' and he shrugs, 'so we kept it casual.'

'You don't need to explain.'

104

'No, but I feel like I should. It's one reason I didn't want you to think badly of me. Jenny was not as innocent as she made out she was and only had Charlie for appearance's sake. He was the decent boyfriend she used as a respectable front and they had that whole cute couple thing going on.'

I'm curious. 'Respectable front?'

He sighs. 'In reality, she liked her sex life several shades darker than Charlie provided.' I'm full of pity for Charlie and hope even more he will come through this okay. I also don't fully understand what Harry meant.

'Several shades darker?'

'Yeah, you know, she enjoyed being tied up an' that.'

Actually, I didn't know, and he looks as uncomfortable talking about this stuff as I am hearing it.

I'm not sure what to say, being distinctly vanilla in my tastes, but the image that springs to mind is of the row of darker bruises left on Jenny's neck. I hadn't given them much thought, given the grander scale of the horror they were buried in and I nearly go to mention them, to ask if they were something to do with this hidden side of Jenny but Pattison's warning comes back to me and I bite back my words.

'Oh.' I say, instead.

'Sorry to be the one to tell you. I know how close you were to her.' *And yet I hadn't seen this, or in any way suspected it.* It occurs to me that maybe Jan had discovered something, which is what she was worried about on Boxing Day. Not for the first time I wish I'd called for that coffee, feel guilty all over again for not doing so, but I put my thoughts about Jan to one side and guide us back to his situation.

'And now they've got some evidence against you?' He looks away.

'In her bed, they found a hair,' and he runs his fingers up through the tousled mess on his head. This conversation makes me uncomfortable, but not as uncomfortable as I'd have been if we were now talking about his semen, as I know they'd found that. I've never spoken to him about his love life before. Why would I have done? Girlfriends had come and gone over the years and we'd double dated when Matt was alive, but that was the closest we'd come to discussing anything like this.

'They were obviously happy to let you go though. That's a positive.' I switch off the yard lights and we go through the gate, stand in the near dark, only a distant street lamp giving us anything to see by.

'Yeah. They gave me a bit of a hard time for not being as open as I should have been with them before. But I told them what our relationship was about and we went through when I'd last been with her and that seemed to satisfy them, at least for now,' he adds ominously, then looks shifty as he turns towards me. 'You might as well know I don't think I'm the only one.'

'The only one?'

'Having sex with Jenny.' He clears his throat. 'There's no way she'd settle for only me and Charlie. That I know.'

And as he walks off home, I'm left wondering if I knew her at all.

We gather outside Number 9 later that evening. There's no sign of the Jacksons' wider family. I didn't think there would be. It's too soon for them, and they live at a distance. This is for the village. The neighbours. The friends. The close-knit community. The villagers walk from all corners of the village to converge on School Lane. I'm glad it's dark. It makes it harder to see who's here, or to be spotted, and Seb and I keep well back, with Harry, who caught up with us on the road. But there's no sign of Pip. We carry tea lights in jam jars like many of the others. Seb has also brought a blanket for reasons unknown to me. I see Pattison and Barker. I see them watching the crowd. The thought the killer might be among us is creepy. But no one challenges them. A television crew films from further down the lane, which fills with flickering lights that bob and weave like fireflies. The vicar eventually says a few words to the near silent crowd. A hundred times the number he speaks to in church. We bow our heads in prayer for our friends. I hear sobs, see those close by wiping tears from eyes. The night is ice cold, the wind bitter. Despite my thick coat, I shiver and Seb, always one step ahead, drapes the blanket across my shoulders. I hold the edges tight around me and smile gratefully at him.

As people return home as quietly as they came, they leave their candles behind, until a sea of twinkling lights covers the verge.

11: Behind Bars.

They formally charge Charlie with the murders of all four members of the Jackson family the following morning. The police had more time left to question him but apparently didn't need it, the DNA evidence all that was required to seal his fate. He was the one who'd had sex with her on the thirtieth. The semen left behind proved it. Not that I imagine he'd have denied it when asked, anyway.

It's still a leap to me. Having sex, then killing the poor girl. But of course, I don't know the full facts. Or, as it turns out, much about any of the people around me.

DS Barker phones me to let me know out of courtesy. I end the call and stare at my phone. I am in the yard hosing Bertie's legs and come to a complete halt. It's Harry's hand on my shoulder that makes me realise he's talking to me. He asks again, 'What's wrong?'

'It's Charlie. They've charged him.' Harry looks as shocked as I feel. 'I'm afraid for him in prison, Harry. He's not strong enough.' He shakes his head and doesn't have to say a word.

Water is pouring across the yard. I look at the hose in my hand. Can't work out why it's there. Harry takes it from me and turns off the tap. He guides me into the tack room and sits me down on one of the storage boxes while he makes us a coffee. We drink in silence, no words necessary.

It's late morning and, leaving the others to get on, I drive to Sally's to see if there is anything I can do. There isn't, obviously, but I want to offer my support. So, after I make my way through the television crews and reporters now blocking access to the cul-de-sac, her tear-stained face peers round the edge of the drawn curtains when I knock and she comes to let me in.

I'm not sure how the media finds out things so fast, but they already know the news and I ignore all the questions they throw at me as I pass.

I hug Sally once the door is closed and feel her shudder as more tears fall.

'I'm so sorry.' She can't speak, so I lead her into the house to find Ned is already there.

'Hi, Ned, you okay?'

'Yeah, I popped in to check on Sal, then she got the news.' He looks like a man way, way out of his comfort zone as he sits perched on the arm of the sofa as though about to make a quick getaway.

I sit Sally down and tell Ned to keep her company while I go to make them both a cup of tea. Ned is the local handyman, although he actually lives several miles away. He always does a good job, so word of mouth has built him a solid business around here and he's often to be found working in Melton. *No job too small*, it says on his van and once, when we'd got into conversation when he was repainting my kitchen, he'd told me he preferred it that way. "The big boys can take the cake", he'd said, in broad Yorkshire. "I'm happy with a lick of the icing and a couple of cherries on the top. That'll do me". He's in his fifties and well-weathered from outside work, his walnut skin accentuating the silver of his hair. He's always working. He's even in his overalls now. I have a quick look in the fridge and pull together a ham sandwich, which I take through on a plate. I doubt she's eaten any time recently.

She shakes her head as I place it in front of her. 'I don't think I could.' Ned has an arm around her shoulders and reaches out his other hand to bring the plate closer.

'Try,' I urge her, 'Charlie won't want you making yourself ill.' The mere mention of his name brings on another bout of sobs.

She looks so frail and, there being nothing of her at the best of times, she's thinner than when I last saw her, but she picks up half of the sandwich and Ned removes his arm, giving her some space. I can see she doesn't want to, but at least she tries, nibbling at a corner, taking ages before she swallows it. I encourage her to drink the tea and I would have been happy to sit in silence with her, but with Ned there it feels awkward.

'It's quite a tussle getting to the front door, isn't it?' I ask for something to say as much as anything.

'I wouldn't know about that. I came in the back way,' and he gesticulates to the garden. Looking out, I can see a gate at the end of the garden.

I sit with her for a couple of hours, eventually discussing the hearing taking place tomorrow. I offer to go with her. She gratefully accepts. I wonder if I can arrange for some other friends to support her there too, so she doesn't feel quite so alone. The phone rings frequently: She lets it go to answerphone. Mostly it's reporters calling, sometimes friends and on those occasions, she picks up. I realise I don't have to arrange anything after all as they also offer to go with her. People are generally kind, especially in a crisis.

As I head back to The Stables, I realise I've missed lunch and go straight into the house.

'Have you been to see Sally again?' asks Seb, and I wonder if he's annoyed by my neighbourly interest.

'They charged Charlie this morning.'

'Harry told me when I went to find out where you'd got to. I noticed your car had gone.'

'Sorry. DS Barker called, and I thought I'd better go straight away.'

'Evidently. Anyway, come and sit for a few moments and have something to eat before you start work again. You'll never get through the afternoon otherwise.' He smiles at me, puts an arm around my waist and pulls me close enough to plant a kiss on my temple. I'm relieved. We've never been an argumentative couple, but this situation has naturally increased the tension around here and between us.

Seb guides me over to the table and sits me down. He unveils a sausage roll and a bowl of soup, which he quickly turns to warm again in the microwave.

'Have you been to the shop?' I ask, eyeing the sausage roll suspiciously.

'Yes, I thought we could do with a change.' He removes the bowl from the microwave and carries it over.

'I bet Sharon was having a field day in there with the news.'

'I couldn't tell you as the daughter served me. Daisy, is it?'

'That's right. Sixteen, going on twenty-six.'

'She's only sixteen. Bloody hell.' He's right, you'd never know. Daisy, another child I've known all her life, is what one would call precocious. Now, at the tender age of sixteen, she is never seen in anything less than full makeup. Sharon told me once, proudly, that she took great interest in makeup and her appearance and she certainly always looks magazine model ready. And subsequently far older than her years. I suspected Sharon had aspirations of her being a model, but I'd heard from Jan one day that Sharon was fixated on her becoming a WAG.

111

I'd had to look that up. It's an acronym for Wives and Girlfriends, apparently, predominantly those of famous footballers. Although no particular target had been specified, as yet. I don't know if Daisy is in on this ambition or if it is purely her mother's desire. Whichever, I think it's a shame she dolls herself up as she does because she is naturally pretty anyway, and the added layer of sophistication is, I feel, out of place when serving behind the counter of a village shop. Although perhaps she is hoping that one day a coachload of famous footballers will pass through and stop off for a pasty.

'How is Sally anyway?' he asks once he's settled in the seat opposite me.

'Devastated.' I decide to tell him the rest of it now. It's easier while we're on the subject. 'He's due in court tomorrow and I said I'd go with her to offer some support.' He reaches out and squeezes my hand.

'That's kind of you. I'm sure she'll appreciate it,' and as simply as that any remaining atmosphere between us evaporates and I'm relieved that in at least one area of my life everything is back to normal.

12: Oddballs.

The next morning, I drive to pick Sally up, and have to crawl past the remaining reporters in the cul-de-sac. There are fewer than before, but I feel sure the rest will only have decamped as far as the court. A couple of Sally's friends are waiting with her, which I'm pleased about, and we agree to travel in my vehicle. The journey is silent, no one in the mood for small talk. Sally sits in the passenger seat staring out of the window, her fingers restless in her lap.

Charlie stands in the dock like a kid dressed up in his dad's clothes. His collar too big, his tie sombre. Pale, he stares straight ahead. I can see his hands shake. It breaks my heart so I can't imagine what it does to his mother. The hearing is short and, as pre-warned by Charlie's solicitor Steve, Charlie is remanded in custody without bail due to the severity of the crime. The decision made, I wrap my arm around Sally's shoulders and she collapses into me, whimpering in distress when he is led away, the only point at which he looks over at her.

Afterwards, we meet with Steve. I leave it for him to speak to Sally while I move to a discreet distance. I know he'll be doing all that is necessary to get Charlie out and Sally tells us on the way home he's already organising for Charlie to be protected in prison as a vulnerable adult on remand and arranging for her to visit him while Steve works on Charlie's defence.

The village is alive with the news when we arrive back, the gossip grapevines pulsating thick and fast, poisoning minds and tarnishing reputations. There are those in the village who feel vindicated in their previously voiced suspicions, and I can't bear to go into the shop to see Sharon's gloating face. I'm sure she'll be making the most of the fact her Eric is in the clear. *I'll sleep safer in my bed knowing he's no longer prowling the streets;* that's what she'd said about Charlie and I wonder how many others in the village have the same beliefs and genuinely feel safer today.

Once I drop Sally and her friends off, I travel back into town to visit a supermarket instead of opting for convenience. I do Sally's shopping at the same time. Her boss has given her compassionate leave for a couple of weeks and I hope, for her sake, the truth will be uncovered by then. In the meantime, the friends and I have swopped numbers so we can keep in touch and make sure we are checking in with her regularly.

The Jacksons' wider family arrives the next day. I know both sides well, so John's brother had called me a few days ago to say they wanted to come down. Would I meet them at the property? I could hardly say no, but hope they have no intention of entering the house, as I certainly can't do that. It's bad enough having to see the family as it is.

Both sets of parents are still alive and want to visit to say a goodbye. I can't imagine how hard it must be for them. This tear in the natural order. Losing your children is one terrible thing, losing your grandchildren too, quite another. Utterly heartbreaking. There is no sign of the bodies being released yet either, so I suppose this visit will have to suffice until they can arrange funerals.

I am the first to arrive. It is a dry and still day, but cold enough for my breath to come out in clouds on the air, and I am wrapped up. Each time I've ridden past over the last week, more flowers have joined those outside the property. Whichever horse I've been on has shied out into the road, some more dramatically than others, suspicious of the unusual sight. Flowers and other mementos now cover the verge to each side of the driveway and I thought, at least, that sight would hearten the family. A visible sign people care.

I knew Seb had laid a bouquet on our behalf too. He'd come home with it from a florist in town, which was a kind gesture, but as I was still a person of interest to the media at the time, I'd asked him to come down to lay them outside the house on his own. It felt like it would be a less poignant moment if the press had been yelling questions at me at the same time.

While I wait, I read the messages. I recognise many names from the village. There are others too, I guess, from schoolfriends. Loopy hearts and angst poured out over the notes. Teddies and other soft toys lie among the flowers. Helium balloons float above.

Pattison and Barker are next. They park past the house and walk back. Hands deep in the pockets of their overcoats. When they draw close, we exchange greetings and they, like me, study the carpet of flowers at their feet. It doesn't appear they are going to speak, so I do.

'Any breakthroughs in the investigation? Other than locking up the wrong man.'

'According to you, Laura, everyone we've spoken to so far is innocent. Yet someone committed this terrible crime and we believe we have the right man.' Pattison's pointed remark hits home and I feel my cheeks flush. He's right, I have defended those around me, because that's what I do, but I do so for a good reason. I know they are innocent and believe the police should look further afield.

'Maybe I have been defensive, but perhaps not everyone you've spoken to is as innocent as they've made out.'

He raises his eyebrows. 'You have something to tell me?'

'Gary Sykes.'

'What about him?'

'Have you scrutinized him?'

'We've spoken to him.'

'But have you properly checked him out? Because he's just the sort to do something like this.'

'*He's just the sort.* What's that supposed to mean?' I count the points off on my fingers.

'He's never had a girlfriend. He's a loner. He's a regular at the pub, so would have known Jenny. He followed me around for a while. Maybe he was pestering her?'

'Do you have any proof, because no one's so much as hinted at that type of behaviour from him in all our questioning?'

'No. Not really.' My mind is whirling but I can't think of anything concrete that might persuade him, so blurt out, 'But he practically stalked me when I first lost Matt.'

'Did you make a complaint at the time?'

'No. I didn't want to approach the police after all they'd already put me through.'

'Did you mention it to anyone else?'

'No…' I hesitate, my discomfort plain in that one word. Pattison raises one eyebrow at me in question. Already defeated, I say, 'I told Harry.' His shoulders slump. 'He was the only one I spoke to.'

'He's hardly in a position to be a reliable witness at the moment now, is he?' I don't know what else I can add to make my point and I'm frustrated that he isn't taking my suggestion seriously, merely knocking me back each time with his questions.

'What about Eric Beesley then?'

'What about him?'

'He's obviously someone you're interested in more than most, and another oddball. You kept him in overnight. Are you sure he's innocent?' Pattison looks puzzled, doesn't respond, but turns and exchanges looks with Barker, who appears equally confused.

'We did?' Now it's my turn to be bewildered. Maybe I'm the one who misunderstood.

'I thought so. At least that's what I understood the situation was. Maybe I've got it wrong…' My voice trails away as I think through what I know.

He is stern when he next speaks. 'Look, Laura. You can't go around accusing random people without any proof and you've given me none of that.' He leans closer to me. 'Not even if they are, in your words, "oddballs".' Heat comes to my face as I realise how badly my behaviour smacks of desperation and that I've now embarrassed myself and probably lost any credibility I might have had with the police.

I scrabble around for some nugget of information that would be of use, but come up with nothing. I feel even more awkward as each silent second passes, but he's not finished with me yet. 'Let me ask you something. Did Harry tell you they were short-staffed at the pub on New Year's Eve because Jenny didn't arrive for work?'

'No. Well, he told me they were short-staffed, but not that it was Jenny who hadn't turned up.'

'The text messages on her phone make for some interesting reading.'

'Why?'

'Because there isn't one from Harry asking where she is.'

'Maybe someone else texted her. Like Mike. He's the landlord, after all.' There I go, defending him again.

'But Harry was her lover. And there are plenty of other messages from him, but none on that night.'

'He was busy behind the bar. It was New Year's Eve.' And again.

'Maybe. Or maybe he already knew there was no point in texting. Maybe he already knew he'd not get an answer.' He fixes me with a look that sends a chill like ice water slithering down my spine. But I grit my teeth and fight back.

'And you said you believed you had the right man?' I send him a glare to match his own.

'Here we go,' says Barker, who straightens from reading the messages on the flowers and looks up the road. Four cars approach at a funereal pace, preventing any further response from Pattison, and I wish I was anywhere but here. Particularly with this new information. Why didn't Harry tell me it was Jenny who hadn't turned up that evening? And why did Pattison bring this up with me when supposedly they have their man? They'd said they'd still be investigating, so perhaps this was it, them following up on inconsistencies.

But another thought occurs to me. Are the police only holding on to Charlie to make the real culprit think they've got away with it? To make them take a misstep? Would they do that?

The next hour is painful. All the extended family have come, and I share hugs and condolences with them. They must have known I'd been the one who found the bodies, but thankfully no one asks me about that. Neither do they want to go inside

Number 9, which Pattison tells me is still a crime scene anyway and therefore sealed off.

Instead we go round to the back garden, out of view of the few nosy neighbours who'd left their houses to watch the gathering, and come together in mourning on the large patio. From there we can see all the way up the garden and into my paddock beyond. There are a few of the ponies grazing, but even though the hedge and trees are bare of leaves, they still provide enough of a screen for me to find it difficult to tell which ones are currently in view. I squint and believe it's Badger, Larney, Donald, and, most likely, Misty. He's never far from wherever Donald is.

When I glance through the French doors, it's hard not to remember all the times I'd been here in happier times. John liked nothing more than to get a barrel in and invite everyone round for a barbeque. I could picture them even now. John, his face red from a combination of ale and the heat from the coals. Jan producing salads and puddings, apparently effortlessly, and joining us for drinks. The girls, in their younger years, skittering in between us all with offered plates of food. In later years, more circumspect, happy to be on the periphery and keen to indulge in the Pimm's that Jan made by the jugful. I realise I have a smile on my face at the memory and drop it rapidly.

'It's all right,' Jan's mother says, placing her hand on my arm. 'It's difficult to be here,' she sweeps her arm round, 'and not remember the happy times.' I nod, unable to speak, her kind words making me choke up once more.

Someone has brought two large flasks of coffee. Someone else a bottle of whisky, along with disposable cups. All appreciate the alcohol-infused winter warmer as the January cold penetrates multiple layers of clothing.

Eventually, John's brother says a few words about the people who brought these two families together. Jan's father speaks equally movingly on behalf of their side. The two police officers and I are the outsiders and stand back while the family does what they need to help them heal. Attention does finally fall on the detectives who face questions about the case and the fact they've arrested Charlie. I can see the families are as perplexed about him being the perpetrator as I am. Jenny and he had been going out for over a year, so all the family had met him. They are of the same opinion. He couldn't have done it.

DI Pattison defends their arrest staunchly, but reassures the family they are still investigating. Questioning other men in the area, following up on the forensic work. Checking out inconsistencies. Exactly as I'd thought.

I trudge home and consider the police case. I know detectives always need to find the means, motive and opportunity for any crime. Here, clearly, Charlie had the opportunity. I am yet to discover a motive, whichever way I look at it. He appears to have been in love with Jenny. Why would he kill her? What would be in it for him to have done so? Regarding means, I guess if, for whatever reason, he'd gone to Jenny's house armed with a knife, that answers that one. But the police have never mentioned a weapon or if they'd found one. Surely this would need to connect back to Charlie either by DNA or by tracking down where he bought it from.

I pause where School Lane meets Main Road, and call Pattison.

'You've never mentioned the weapon,' I say as he answers.

'Hello to you too, Laura.'

'Have you found it?' I persevere and wonder if he'll tell me anything.

'We haven't, no.'

'So you can't link Charlie to the crime by that?'

'We have his DNA at the scene, Laura, and he's admitted he was there.' I can tell I'm trying his patience. 'We are still looking for the weapon, but we already know what the killer used.'

'What?'

'A knife from Jan's knife block. There's one missing.'

Damn it.

'Which Charlie would have had access to.' I don't realise I've spoken out loud until I get Pattison's response.

A dry, 'Indeed.' *Along with any other person in the house that night*, I think as I hang up and carry on my journey.

With opportunity and means covered, I come back to motive. What motive would Charlie have had to kill Jenny? To everyone who knew him, he appeared the doting boyfriend. But then you never knew exactly what was going on inside another person's head. I think back to what Harry told me about his relationship with Jenny. What if Charlie had found out about that? Or about whoever else she had been running with. Could that have pushed him over the edge? Sent him temporarily insane, perhaps? Because if it was him, and jealousy had momentarily blinded him, killing Jenny was one thing. But also we have to believe he'd murdered the rest of her family. Surely no one in their right mind could do that. Thinking these traitorous thoughts about Charlie causes me discomfort because as I still believe he is innocent, casting any doubt on that makes me feel guilty.

13: Mysterious Girl.

At the beginning of the third week of January, I'm riding Fifty back up School Lane towards home when, in the distance, I see a girl standing on the opposite verge to Number 9 staring at the property. She's on the skinny side of slim, shoulders slightly hunched as if she's not strong enough to square them, long dark hair that hangs like curtains, and she's transfixed on something about the house. The police tape is still in place but, now broken in a couple of places, the tatty ends hang down on this still day. I get closer. The noise of us approaching does nothing to distract her from her focus. Until, that is, I call out to her.

'Hey, are you okay?' Then I immediately regret it.

She jumps like a startled rabbit at my voice, as though it's broken her trance, and turns away from me scrabbling for her car door.

I stop, hoping she might too. 'Don't go. Did you know Jenny?' She looks about her age. She ignores me, climbing quickly into the car before slamming the door and driving off in a hurry. I haven't seen her around here before and wonder why she's come now. I curse myself for scaring her off. She could, of course, simply have been a friend leaving flowers, but there was something about the fact she couldn't get away from me fast enough that I found curious. Like I had caught her out.

Or she knew something.

That's it! I decide, as I mull over the strange girl's disappearance. She must know something. Why else would she run?

When I arrive at the yard, the place is in chaos, which pushes any further thoughts about the girl from my mind for now. A local private school brings a small busload of pupils over for lessons during term time and while it's perfectly usual to have one issue during a session, today there had been three, which involved several still tearful children. Pooh had stood on one girl's foot, and she is still howling. Scrapes, who didn't get his name at random, had shot through the opening door to the arena when there wasn't enough of a gap for both him and his rider. He'd thereby smacked one leg of his jockey hard enough against the frame to ensure a sizeable bruise would appear over the next day or two. The child had, however, stayed on, so that was something, even if she was now limping. Finally, Zodiac had taken off with one of the better riders (who was without stirrups at the time) and jumped over a small fence which was not part of the planned activities for that morning's class, before depositing his jockey unceremoniously on the ground. At least it was in the arena which, being a sand and rubber mix, cushioned the fall.

Pip looks frazzled and is debriefing the teacher accompanying the children when I appear.

I speak to him too, and being of a practical nature, he's absolutely fine with the situation.

'No bones broken,' he says, 'and a few stories to tell once they've got over the shock.' While we have risk assessments in place, I like his attitude; it's one reason we work with the school in the way we do. There have been others who have wanted lessons but also for us to provide a risk-free environment for their charges: no way could we consider doing that.

Soon, everyone is smiling again and happily untacking their ponies, putting them in the small stalls: that is part of their lesson here. They do some of the grooming, learn how to tack and untack, a bit extra than the average riding lesson. Plus, it

123

means Pip isn't left holding the reins of ten or more ponies at the end of the session. I realise, as we get on with sorting the children and ponies out, how much easier it is having people around who are largely unaware of the recent tragedy, or who at least aren't bringing it up all the time like the locals; it makes for a refreshing change.

I put Fifty away and go back to give Pip a hand, both of us breathing a sigh when the school party has gone and the yard is quiet again. Pip has a few hours now in which to ride Pegasus before the after-school lessons begin. This is a lucrative, if hard, business Pip is running. Once again, I have my mother to thank for having the foresight to put up such a large indoor arena and equip it with lighting. This means lessons are possible in all weathers and after darkness has fallen, which makes a tremendous difference to the business.

Once the yard has settled down again, my thoughts drift back to the mysterious girl outside Number 9. I don't know how to find out who she is or where she comes from. If it is Jenny's school, which is most likely, I know it has over two thousand pupils. Probably only three hundred in the sixth form, though. I wonder if the school will give me the details of a girl if I described her to them. Nowadays, I am pretty sure they wouldn't, not with data protection being as stringent as it is. I contemplate asking Daisy, Sharon and Eric's daughter, about her. Despite the age gap, she might recognise who I'm talking about, but I decide against it. I know I'm unlikely to get Daisy on her own and Sharon would be all over why I'm asking, which I can't bear.

The good thing about having a physical job is that I have plenty of time to think. The bad thing about having a physical job is that I have plenty of time to think. Which only means that today all that occupies my mind is the mystery girl and what her interest in Number 9 might be.

14: Hunting Down a Schoolgirl.

The next morning, I still can't get the girl out of my head. What if she knows something? The way she ran from me made me fairly certain that's the case. Why would she take off like that if she had nothing to hide? I make a point of going down School Lane on every ride out over the next few days in the hope she returns, but there is no sign of her. Eventually, I decide to take some action. I ask Harry if he'll do afternoon stables the next day, which is the Friday. I have some business to attend to.

The following afternoon, I drive into town and head for the comprehensive on the outskirts. It is the school both Jenny and Judy had attended, as had I, many years ago. I find a parking space in the packed car park. Getting out, I lock my car. Then I walk up and down the rows, trying to spot the vehicle the girl had driven off in. In hindsight, my task would have been easier had I taken down the number plate. Unfortunately I hadn't, being more interested at the time in the girl's reaction and the reason for her being there. I'm also not great at recognising the different cars. I know the one I seek is small, silver and old, but these appear to be common features shared by many of the cars here. Eventually I come across one that fits the bill, plus it has stickers on the back window. Something I had remembered. Although looking round at a few of the other cars, stickers are abundant in most, along with soft toys that line the parcel shelves and peer out like the front row of a theatre audience. There are only a few students about currently, skipping out early as sixth formers are wont to do. I glance at my watch. It's nearly time for the end of school bell to ring and I'm happy to wait.

In the dwindling light of a winter's day, I look again at the stickers in the back window. A mish mash of emojis which must say something, but their meaning is lost on me. A couple look music related but are for bands I've never heard of. And a sticker I've seen before, but can't remember where. On a dark purple background, there is a black circle. In that are three black symmetrical shapes made to look like they're moving round with purple dots like an eye in each. Odd. I can't fathom what it means.

I hear the school bell and go to lean against the tree next to the car, if it is her car. I don't want to appear to be invading the girl's space. A constant stream of students exit the main gate. The older ones start across the car park, loading backpacks and bags into cars before getting in and driving off. The car park empties rapidly by those keen to get home. Unfortunately, the person I want is not among them. I debate whether to retrieve my car from the other side of the car park so I'll have somewhere warm to sit, but worry that the minute I'm out of sight she will appear and I'll miss my opportunity. I stick it out. She might have an after-school activity of some sort. Most of the teachers' cars have gone by now too and I'm thankful no one's questioned why I am here. It is dark and I am cold, walking round in circles and stamping my feet to keep warm. I curse the fact I hadn't gone to get my car when I'd thought about it earlier. I tell myself I'll wait until half-past five and if there is still no sign, I'll leave and try another day. As it happens, I don't have to wait that long. Shortly after five out she comes, a large art portfolio tucked under one arm. I recognise the long dark hair, which shines black like wet tarmac under the inadequate lighting.

I don't want to frighten her, so make my presence obvious by stepping away from the tree and out into the roadway. I see her pace falter when she spots me, but she clearly doesn't see me as a threat and carries on towards her car. She doesn't question why I am there but makes her way to the boot and unlocks it, placing her portfolio inside. I haven't properly thought through what I am going to say to her, so start with, 'Hello.'

She glances at me as though it only occurs to her right then she's the reason I'm here, and looks away without answering. Makes for the driver's door.

'Please, don't go. I've been waiting to speak to you.'

'Why? I don't know you.' She pulls open the door. I stretch out a hand.

'You were outside Jenny's house,' I blurt out, hoping to make her stop. It works. She turns towards me. Dressed entirely in black, she's more made up than she was the other day. A fringe like a pelmet, big dark eyes heavily rimmed in a pale face, dark lipstick. She wears a plain black choker.

'Who are you?'

'Laura. I was on the horse.' Recognition crosses her face, but she says nothing further. 'I'm a friend of the family. I own the riding school round the corner.' She raises her chin slightly. 'You were a friend of Jenny's?' She shrugs, which is not as positive a reaction as I was after, so I try with the main reason I'm here. 'Look,' and I hesitate, 'Sorry, I don't know your name.' She isn't forthcoming with it, so I blunder on. 'I don't know why you were outside the house, but I thought you might know something.'

'Like what?'

'I don't know. That's why I'm here, to find out.'

'Police have already got someone for it.'

'Charlie? He wouldn't hurt a fly.' I gaze at her. There's a moment of connection, then I say, 'but then I think you already suspect that. I don't think it was him either, but I also don't know if the police are seriously looking any further. If there's something you know, tell them.' She shakes her head and gets in the car.

'They wouldn't listen.'

'Try me, I'll listen.' She stares at me as if trying to decide.

'Can't talk, I've got to get to work.' She moves to pull the door closed. I grab it with my hand and see the flash of annoyance on her face.

'What about tomorrow? Can we meet for a coffee?'

'I've got to get to work.' This time she means business. The door rips out of my hand as she slams it. Seconds later, she drives off. Disappointed, I make my way back to my car and get in, turning the heater on full blast to thaw myself out before I get home.

I'm irritated I've wasted all that time and found out precisely nothing. Not even her name. I should have been more prepared, and I castigate myself for not having my number on a card or something, so I could have given that to her. At least then, when she'd had some time to think about it, she would have had a way to contact me should she have changed her mind.

I pull into the drive as Harry is leaving via the yard gate. He has Scout with him, walks over to the car and opens my door for me. Scout leaps up at me in excitement, her paws scrabbling at my legs, and I bend down to make a fuss over her.

'Hi, Harry. Sorry for being so long, everything okay?'

'Yup, all okay. Did you get done what you needed to do?'

'Yes, sort of,' but I don't elaborate. I get out of the car, lock it and make my way towards the house. He walks alongside. Seb is away working in London today and he won't be home until late, so the house is shrouded in darkness. Harry comes in with me and between us we get lamps on, curtains drawn and the wood-burning stove lit so the place feels homely again, which relaxes me because I hadn't expected to be out for so long. Harry is familiar with my home, but it's been a while since he's come in for any length of time. Since Seb moved in, actually. They get on but they're not friends, not like he and Matt used to be.

In those days Harry often came round as we'd lived here with my mother, even after we'd married, the house far too big for one person. Plus, it was the best place possible for being on hand for the horses. It made no sense to move anywhere else.

'Do you fancy staying for supper?' I ask Harry as I peer hopefully into the fridge. 'Actually, I'll take that back as the only thing I can make from these remains is cheese on toast.' He smiles, catches himself and it drops from his face.

'No, you're all right. You're welcome to join me at the pub, though. I'm going for a quick bite before the darts match starts. Should be a decent crowd. That lot from the estate are due in.' It probably would be a good evening, but I'd already been out enough for the day.

'No thanks, you enjoy yourself. I'm going to thaw out a ready meal, eat in front of the telly and get an early night.' He gives me a look like he's far from likely to enjoy himself.

'The high spots of Melton too much for you, are they,' he tries to joke, but delivered without his usual exuberance, it falls flat. He makes his way to the back door, pauses, turns to look at me and I raise my eyebrows encouraging him to say whatever's on his mind, but he doesn't, he simply turns back to the door muttering, 'see you tomorrow,' as he lets himself out. I almost call him back, almost go to ask him why he didn't tell me it was Jenny who didn't turn up for work on New Year's Eve, but something holds me back. I put it down to tiredness. I don't have the energy to get into all that right now, especially when I think the police are making something out of nothing, anyway.

I close the fridge, lock the door behind him, and delve into the freezer for something to put in the microwave. Seb told me he would have dinner in town and would be back late, so I eat in front of an early evening quiz show. A short while later he calls, which is unusual. I always imagine I'm the last thing on his mind when he's wining and dining with his work colleagues or fancy London friends.

'Hello. This is a lovely surprise. Is everything all right?'

'Yes, absolutely fine. I'm en route to the restaurant and missing you, so thought I'd see how you are.'

'That's thoughtful, thank you.'

'I know I don't always show it, but you're the most important person in my life, Laura. I suppose the tragedy has brought that home to me, so I'm trying to be more considerate.' There's a smile on my face. I'm sure I take him for granted too, and should do the same. 'How's your day been?' he continues. 'What have you been up to?'

I can't imagine what he thinks I might have been up to other than my usual horse-based activities. 'Nothing out of the ordinary. It's been a quiet one. Harry has gone to the pub for his dinner though, so hopefully he's feeling better. Not that he looks it.'

'I suspect he's feeling the strain of being under police scrutiny. That must be difficult.'

131

'Yes, you're probably right. We'll have to keep an eye on him.'

'Indeed. So, nothing else to tell me?'

'No, I don't think so. Like I say, it's been a quiet one.' I feel slightly guilty but don't mention my trip to the school. When I'd told him I'd seen a girl outside Number 9 earlier in the week he'd dismissed her as a ghoul wanting to relish in the tragedy and I thought he'd think my attempt to track her down today rather amateurish, especially when I'd found out precisely nothing. 'How about you? Had a good day?'

'Yes, all good, and I'm meeting up with a couple of old rugby mates now, so looking forward to having a few drinks. Actually, I'm approaching the restaurant, so I'd best go.'

'Okay. Have a great time and be careful coming home.'

'Always,' he reassures me, and we end the call.

I don't envy his evening out at all and our relationship goes to show how people with different likes and dislikes can live together in perfect harmony, as long as you are respectful of each other's desires. Curling up with Scout to watch a film, I fall asleep in time to miss the ending. When I wake, I check my watch. It's only ten o'clock, but I pull on my boots and a coat, take a torch from its recharging unit and walk with Scout over to the stables to check on the horses. I top up water buckets where needed and am soon back inside, content that all is calm. I take my sleeping pill and make my way to bed secure in the knowledge that once asleep there is no way Seb will disturb me when he comes in, no matter how loud he is.

15: An Extraordinary Night Out.

When I wake, I feel a wave of relief when I realise it's the weekend and I take a moment to consider that. Weekends mean a bit of a break for me. Owners come to ride their horses and many like to do the horse management too, all of which means less for me to do. Running the yard is no picnic in the depths of winter but, as Seb has quipped a few times over recent months, it's not like I have to do it. He tells me he earns enough to keep us and selling the yard would allow us an early retirement. I commented on the fact that he is fifteen years older than me and at thirty-four I wasn't quite ready to consider retiring yet. I hadn't even had the family I'd once planned. He'd grown quiet, said maybe we should work on that. When he'd joked that neither of us were getting any younger, I'd said yes, maybe we should. We've been trying ever since in a low key, relaxed kind of way, not that there's been any success yet.

Like me, Seb has already been married and had been through what sounded like a hideously acrimonious divorce from his ex, Tilly, a couple of years before I met him. They had a teenage son together, Toby, who I have not yet met, despite Seb and I having been married for over two years.

I look at him now, lightly snoring on the pillow across from mine, full lips slightly parted. He's sensitive about his approaching fiftieth and I don't think the age gap helps that, but he looks younger and keeps himself fit, using the gym at his club in town and going for the occasional run. He complains about the lines at the corners of his eyes but to me they only add an attractive crinkle to his blue-eyed smile. In my eyes, and frankly in the eyes of many among my acquaintance, he has

133

nothing to worry about. I have seen how flirtatious women become in his presence – even the odious Sharon, who, like a cat on heat, couldn't get enough of him at last year's Barn Dance. I feel privileged he chose me to be with.

We'd had a whirlwind romance, having met by chance when Seb had been passing through the area and broken down some way from the village. I'd come across him trying to pick up a mobile signal in the middle of nowhere and, having no signal either (not unusual in this part of the country) had ridden swiftly home to get help. He'd called to thank me and the rest, as they say, is history.

I lost Matt first, then my mother only a couple of years after that. So, I'd been alone for two years rattling around in a too big house, work my only focus, and Seb had come along at precisely the right time, picking me up from the low, and lonely, point I was in. I hadn't imagined I'd ever be happy again, but he had changed all that. We got married six weeks later. Initially, I'd baulked at the speed our relationship moved at, but he'd been passionate about the romance of it all and I loved him enough to be swept along with the whirlwind. I'd only grown to love him more since.

He told me, from the start, his son had taken the divorce badly, and him finding someone else so soon made it even worse. Therefore, it was best to give it some time before we met, but I have wondered how much more time he is going to need. Meanwhile, I'm also incredibly thankful Seb is happy to consider having a second family with me. Not all men would be up for that.

I get up without disturbing him and gather my clothes together before I tiptoe out. Showering quickly, I dress and go downstairs to let a happy-to-see-me Scout out to relieve herself.

While I have a glass of juice and a banana, I look out of the kitchen window at the pitch black, which doesn't make the long working days any easier to deal with. Dark mornings and evenings make this time of year depressing and I daydream for a moment or two, allowing myself to imagine being on a golden beach, warm sunshine on my skin, or lying on a sun lounger, with a pool close by to dive into should it get too warm. What a problem to have. I shake myself out of my reverie and decide I should make time for a holiday this year. As Seb's birthday is approaching, maybe I should book something like that for him as his present. I know he'd love it. He is forever going on about getting away more often, or even at all. Resolving to look into it later, I make my way over to the yard to start the daily routine.

I am back in for breakfast at nine and am surprised to see Seb up, dressed and eating toast. Often after a night out in London, he sleeps in for hours.

'Morning, you're up and about early.'

'Yes, damned nuisance, actually. Mother's called and the old man's had a fall. I need to see them, I'm afraid.'

'Oh, okay. Is he all right?'

'She says he's fine. A bit shaken but nothing broken, apparently. Still, they want me to go and I thought I'd better, you know how it is.'

'Yes, absolutely. You must go. Do you want me to come?'

'No, no. That's unnecessary. I know you have a lot on here.'

'It is the weekend, I could get the others to cover.'

'Don't bother them. I'm sure they have enough to do,' he says, brushing the crumbs from his hands. 'I'll pop up today, stay over to reassure them everything's fine and be back tomorrow. All right?' He ends brightly, like it's all sorted and I agree because his mind's obviously made up. I wouldn't mind a trip to see his parents, though. I've only met them once, and that was at a restaurant halfway between us after our marriage in a registry office. It was as low-key a wedding as you can get, but at the time felt wildly spontaneous and romantic.

He leaves the table to get himself ready, and I am left to my own thoughts. An idea comes to mind that might solve the issue of me never getting to see his parents. Forget the holiday. I could plan a surprise gathering for Seb's birthday, maybe even get his son to come along. Hmm, I decide I'm going to have to give it some thought, but I quickly warm to the idea. While I'm not sure that he'd appreciate a full-blown party, a small family get-together at a decent restaurant would mark the occasion in a manner more fitting to recent events.

Of course, involving Toby would mean me having to contact Tilly discreetly, and we've never spoken before. I'll have to give that some thought, too.

Seb bounces back down the stairs and heads for the back door only minutes later and is so eager to check all is well with his parents, he almost forgets to kiss me on the way out.

'I'll be back tomorrow,' he says, 'although I'll pop in and have lunch with Tobes on the way back if he's around. Maybe then you and I can have a relaxed evening in together with a bottle of wine and get on with the baby-making.' I smile, appreciating the effort when he's being torn in all directions. Toby is at a boarding school between here and my parents-in-law and Seb tries to get to see him every weekend that Toby isn't otherwise occupied on a sports field somewhere. He does an amazing number of sports and activities, though, and Seb told me he was that sort of kid and always had to be doing something. I'd suggested he might like to come here and try his hand at riding, which could be an ice breaker between us, but he hasn't taken up that suggestion so far.

Once Seb has gone, I decide to follow up on another idea I'd had while mucking out earlier. I wrap up warmly again and walk round to Number 9. Everything is much as it was two weeks ago. The police tape is still up but is becoming more tattered in places. The flowers, soft toys and balloons remain in place, the cold keeping the flowers fresher than they might otherwise have been by now. I wonder who will eventually deal with clearing all this away and how long is a decent enough period to leave it here, anyway.

I duck under the tape and approach Jenny's car. I still haven't placed where I'd seen that sticker in the back of Jenny's as yet unnamed friend's vehicle, but I know Jenny shared the same fondness for decorating her back window so thought I'd have a look. Sure enough, there it is, hidden right in the window's corner and overshadowed by the others around it. Inspecting it now I have proper daylight to see it by, I can pick out that there is a cross in the background. I peer closer, scrunching my eyes to see better and realise with some surprise that the cross is in fact two whips. I straighten my back and wonder again what this means. There are no words or any other information on the sticker, so it's not as if it's an advert but more like a belonging thing. Like an emblem for a group or club to let others know you're a member, too. The main thing is, though, that it's a link between the two girls other than them only being friends at school. However, I'm not sure how to go about finding out what it is, or was, they belong to. I take a photo of the sticker, check my watch and realise the morning is slipping away and I've still got my horse to ride.

137

Rooster is pure quality, and I adore him. He's fifteen two hands high, a bay thoroughbred cross and an excellent all-rounder happily tackling anything I put in front of him. Often on a Saturday or Sunday I'll get to ride him out on my own and it's then we have some fun and do things I wouldn't risk on someone else's horse. Today is no exception and after warming up, I take to the track that runs along the wall around the estate and open Rooster up into a gallop to blow the cobwebs away. I slow him as we approach the entrance gates and we pass those slowly so I can have a good nosy in, envious as always of the land Emma has to ride over. I cross over to the woods and jump a couple of fallen trees, before heading back towards the village and home. Rooster is loving life, jogging along, his head up and alert. I arrive back at the stables with a smile on my face, which feels strange after so many days of sadness.

'That's good to see,' Harry says as he walks out of the tack room. 'Had a good time?'

'Excellent, thanks. It was much needed.' And that's the truth. It's going to take some time. But the paralysis that has assailed my mind and body has begun to lift. Although, even as I think this, shame washes over me at the fact my life is moving on while someone has snatched the Jacksons' away. The bounce taken out of my step. I lead Rooster back to his stable and untack him before rubbing him down. As always, even though he's clipped out he's become a little heated, and I don't want to rug him up when he's still damp. I give him some time, getting a few jobs done. Once he's calm, I give him a good groom, replace his rugs, and leave him with his hay net.

I make a point of going round each of the stables to check in with all the owners to ensure everything is all right with them. Some have been out, some are still getting ready, everyone is on their own time and there's a good feeling in the yard even if now, like the rest of the village, it inevitably feels muted after the tragedy. Many of the owners know each other, so ride out together and there's good camaraderie in the yard, something I've nurtured by being quite careful over who keeps their horses here. It's not that I can afford to be choosy particularly, but I know from mistakes I've made in the past how bad it can be when there's one difficult owner around. Everyone suffers.

I take a trip up to the indoor arena, and check on the ponies on the way. Some will still be out in the paddock, some currently in a lesson and a few are waiting for lessons later on in the day. I walk along the stalls to see who's in, and find Romeo and Goldie. Taking the opportunity, I check them over and give them a bit of fuss. I stroke Romeo's ears and find myself butted by Goldie's palomino nose, seeking attention too, which makes me smile. Further along are Kelly, Merry Legs, Fella and right at the end and lying down, Princess.

Carrying on my journey with Scout scampering about as I do, I pass by the outdoor menage where one owner is schooling her horse, Candy. We exchange a few words and I leave her to it as I go to check on Pip. I let myself in the small rear door which leads to the viewing gallery and take a seat, quietly greeting the parents who are watching, so as not to distract Pip or her pupils. The parents are wrapped up as from experience they know there is no heating and it doesn't take long at this time of year for the cold to set in when you're sitting around.

I turn my attention to Pip, who is an excellent instructor, and I enjoy watching her lessons. She has a novice group in currently and is playing games to get the children to relax. I stay for the rest of the lesson, which goes smoothly, and I'm pleased to hear the parents muttering complimentary things, plus all the children end the lesson looking like they've enjoyed themselves.

Pip mostly teaches children because of the size of the ponies we have but I know she's been on the lookout for a couple of larger cobs to extend into teaching adults, plus some of the livery owners book her for private tuition so she's always busy.

After I've seen and spoken with everyone I need to I go back to the house for lunch, and while I make a sandwich I power up my laptop and sit to do some investigation. I had the idea when I spotted the matching sticker in Jenny's car window this morning that it might signify a group or club, and I wonder if I can find out anything further online.

I think whatever links Jenny and her friend, it will be local, as they've only recently become independently mobile, so it's unlikely to be anything that far away. Searching for clubs in the nearest town, I get many results and scan through these, but see nothing that strikes me as likely. I think about the whips on the sticker and ponder what that might mean. I wouldn't describe myself as a prude, but neither do I know much about sexual things of a, er… more adventurous nature, having never felt the need. However, I'm reminded of what Harry told me recently about what Jenny liked in bed. Therefore, while my suspicions rise over what this might be about, I could also be completely wrong so as I type *BDSM clubs* into the search bar and hit enter I do so with a certain amount of trepidation as I'm not sure what I'm about to discover.

Gold. As it turns out.

There, as the first result, is a site displaying the same image as on the sticker the girls have in their cars. I check it against the photo on my phone and with some nervousness open the link, prepared to have my mind well and truly broadened. I investigate the website with increasing amazement. Admittedly, there is little on here about the more violent practices, those that I assume would involve the whips shown on the sticker, but there is plenty available on what they offer for those looking to swap partners, engage in orgies or for those who simply prefer to watch, while there are others, apparently, who like to have an audience. I can't help wondering what Jenny and her friend are, or were, involved in. And whether this was what Jan had possibly had suspicions about and wanted to discuss.

I check the directions. The club is called Liberation. It's on the other side of town to Melton and out in the countryside, probably to maintain a little privacy. Set back from the road down a long drive, it looks like a large country house or hotel. It is members only and I wonder what it takes to join. Not much, I discover on further investigation, especially if you're a woman, as they are apparently always welcome, in groups or alone. It says so right there on the website.

I consider this for a moment. Checking the opening times, I wonder if I have the nerve to investigate this club, because I think if I do, I will find Jenny's friend there. I'm keen to discover whatever it is she knows about Jenny. The alternative is waiting until Monday and hanging around the school to speak to her again. That feels the more comfortable option, but perhaps if I track her down somewhere else she will realise I will not give up until she talks to me.

I busy myself with a few other jobs while I mull this over. I waver between feeling excited at having discovered a clue that might shed some light on what caused someone to murder Jenny, and nervous at the bat shit crazy idea of actually going to the club and into a world I'm totally unequipped for.

Late afternoon I go out to the yard to look after all the horses I'm still responsible for, but my thoughts are somewhere else entirely. In fact, Pip has to call my name several times before I realise she's at Rooster's stable door and wants to talk to me.

'Sorry, what?' I say.

'Are you all right? You're away with the fairies.' She has a puzzled expression on her face.

'Yes, sorry,' I say again, 'Bit distracted. How can I help?'

'I wondered if you'd put in the feed order. We're running low.'

'It's coming Monday. I think we've got enough to last until then.'

'Yes, we have, just wanted to make sure some was on the way,' and she is about to move off when she pauses again and turns back. 'Is everything okay, Laura?'

'Fine,' I say, in that too bright a way that only makes it obvious everything is definitely not fine. She narrows her eyes at me, no doubt wondering if she should push the point, but I shoo her away and say she should get on. There's nothing to see here.

When evening stables are done, I hurry over to the house. I've made my mind up and I am keen to get going before it changes again. I feed Scout then, being too nervous to eat, I go straight to my wardrobe to see what I have that would be suitable to wear to a sex club. Nothing, unsurprisingly. My clothing choices stretch barely further than jeans and a variety of tops. But I do have one decent pair of black trousers, a white silk blouse and smart black suede ankle boots. That will have to do, although I can't help wondering if I'll be overdressed, or under, because what exactly is the dress code for such a place?

As I get ready, I gaze out of our bedroom window at the cottages opposite. I see Olivia Croxton pull up in her cottage's driveway, the one next to Maisie's, and get out of her car and her husband Kyle opens the door as she carries bags of shopping in. They're a nice young couple. I can't help but wish my friend Maisie Brooks was at home though. She'd have been more than game to come along with me this evening. Sadly, however, it looks as though she's staying in Spain for the foreseeable future, the *To Let* board prominent outside her place. I think of the great evenings Jan and I had when we went over to hers and have to blink back tears at another reminder of how life has changed. Jan gone. Maisie gone, albeit temporarily. I miss having my girls around to discuss stuff with.

After donning my 'going out' coat as opposed to my work one, I leave the house, my apprehension increasing on the journey. *What if this is one big mistake and the girls had nothing to do with this place, the stickers merely a coincidence? I'll look like a prize prawn then, won't I.*

I travel through the town and out onto country roads on the other side. I don't know this area, having no actual need to come here, but I've only been traveling a few minutes when I see the entrance come up. Turning into it, I continue along the drive. Something else occurs to me. *What if I see someone here I know? Or, someone sees my car and makes some comment to Seb about it being here?* These and many other doubts start crowding my mind. When I reach the end of the drive and turn into the car park, I have to fight the temptation to drive straight back out again.

I park in the darkest corner, furthest away from the house, the front of which is attractively up-lit. I watch as a couple of other cars arrive. They are all fancy here, no run-of-the-mill family saloons or estates. I watch as couples exit their vehicles and walk towards the building, and feel utterly sick. They do all have clothes on, at least that's something, although they're considerably dressier than me. Which isn't difficult.

I release my seatbelt, get out of the car and head for the main entrance. There's a lady on the desk when I enter and, not quite knowing what to do, I ask if I can go in.

'Are you a member?' she says, and I notice she is dressed similarly to me, which about sums me up; I look like staff. Although she also has an electric blue bob, with eye shadow and lipstick to match, and is considerably more striking because of it.

'No.' I manage. 'I haven't been here before, but I was wondering if I could have a trial evening?' Was that likely to even be a thing? My request doesn't faze her, and she dips her head as if in acquiescence and steps out from behind her desk.

'You're brave,' she says over her shoulder as she leads me down a short hallway. 'Women mostly arrive here in packs.' She reaches a door at the end.

'Or foolish,' I mutter. She laughs lightly.

'You'll be all right,' she says as she shows me to the entrance, 'go in, have a drink, and see what you think. If you want to stay and take part in the fun and games this evening, you can do. If it's not for you, call it a night.' She leans in reassuringly, 'If you find it is for you, we can join you up as a member after,' and she ends with, 'The fun starts from ten.'

Ten! I'm usually on the countdown to bed by then!

She keys in a code and pushes the door open to let me in. Wishes me good luck.

The room beyond pulsates purple and black.

By the time the door has fully closed behind me, my eyes have acclimatised and I realise it's not as dark as I first thought, but pleasingly, it is discreet. Large black leather sofas are grouped around low coffee style tables, smaller seats around glossy, higher tables. Jet walls glow purple under subtle lighting. There's a background thrum. Not recognisable music, but a beat. Enough to cover conversation, and set the tone. The scent, were it a perfume, I'd call anticipation. People, little more than shadows, sit talking in pairs or small groups as they drink: and that appears to be all they are doing, which comes as something of a relief.

Alone and unable to see potential predators I'm aware of my vulnerability, so I move confidently, as if I know what I'm doing.

The bar across the room is an oasis of light in the dark, and I make my way directly over to it, feeling vindicated in my decision to come here, because behind it is the very person I've come to find.

It surprises her to see me, although she seems like someone who is rarely surprised by anything. But as I step out of the shadow and into her orbit, she halts in her tracks before continuing to polish the glass she holds as she tries to maintain her cool demeanour and, as I slide onto the predictably black leather bar stool, she asks me what I want to drink.

'I don't.'

'You don't get to talk to me if you're not drinking. That doesn't pay my wages.'

'Something soft. What do you have?'

'A mocktail? Something citrus do you?' I leave the choice in her capable hands, having never had a mocktail before, or a cocktail come to that.

145

The bar is what I imagine one in a smart city to be like, all glass and chrome on the brightly lit back wall, bottles spaced artfully, decoration as well as stock. Hanging lights above the ebony bar top itself scarcely give enough light for the bar person to work by, their spread barely sufficient to reach me but I don't get out much so what do I know, other than the fact I'm way beyond the level where I feel comfortable.

'How did you find me?'

'The sticker in your rear window. Jenny had one too.'

'Good detective work.' She places the mocktail in front of me. It has froth on the top of it.

'I felt it was… a connection.'

A voice behind me says, 'I'll get that,' and a man appears to my right. I hold my hand up to stop him.

'You're all right, I've got this.' He fits the tall, dark and handsome bill, but is a complication I don't need.

'I've been watching you from across the room.'

'Seriously? Well, you go on back over there and keep on watching.' His eyebrows rise, he withdraws his hand and card from the bar but fails to move. I bring my hand up and wave him away with the back of my fingers, 'Go on, shoo.' And, surprisingly, he does.

I look back at Jenny's still unnamed friend, who can barely contain a smile.

'Wow, burn,' she says, like I'm cool or something. 'That'll be ten quid.'

'That'll be what?'

'Ten.'

'I didn't realise I was paying *all* your wages myself.' There's that smile again as I reach into my bag for some cash and almost regret turning down the earlier offer. 'Look, I need to talk to you properly. Can we meet somewhere where we won't get interrupted?'

The darkness summons up another guy who moves the closest bar stool to me even closer, then climbs aboard.

'I watched what you did to him over there,' he says, and he jerks his head towards the back wall where I can see nothing but shadows. 'I bet you can get real tough on a man when you want to.' I'm not sure I care for his tone. 'I haven't seen you here before, have I?'

'No, it's my first time,' I make the mistake of saying.

'How about you buddy up with me and my girl over there,' and he points off to somewhere in the blackness, 'we're planning on some role play later and think you'd be great at keeping us behaving as we should.'

'What?'

'Isn't that what you've got going on here?' and he waves a finger towards my perfectly fine outfit, 'the whole strict teacher dominatrix thing?'

'What?' I'm aware I'm repeating myself and clearly look aghast at the suggestion, so add, 'Bugger off!' to my limited vocabulary. He's taken aback but at least has the good sense not to press me further, sliding off the stool in retreat.

'You're too funny,' comes from across the bar as she mixes another drink.

'Well, honestly.' I'm exasperated. 'Look, I need to get out of here, but not before we've set up a meeting.'

'Okay,' she says, as if in defeat, 'I can see you're determined. Tomorrow at ten. The garden centre café.'

'I will see you there.' I pick up my drink and drain the contents before pointing the glass towards her. 'And don't make me come back here to find you again.' She makes a noise that sounds almost like a laugh and I put the glass down. 'Actually, that's not bad.'

'Why thank you,' and she gives a mock bow. 'It's Unity by the way, my name.' I smile at what feels like a huge step forward.

'Thank you, Unity. I shall see you in the morning,' I say as I climb off my stool. I look over to the back wall and head off towards where I believe the exit is.

Blue hair is still on the door as I'm leaving.

'Not for you?' she says as I pass.

'No, far too tame,' I say, and I release what feels like a long held breath as the cold air hits my face.

16: Toasted Teacakes.

I arrive at the garden centre café a little before ten and make myself comfortable with a coffee at a table that faces the entrance. I think there's a strong probability Unity will be a no-show. As it is, I hardly recognise her when she arrives only a few minutes later, but without her disguise.

It has already occurred to me that considering she'd no doubt had a late night, or early morning, it was surprising she wanted to meet on a Sunday morning. Most teenagers would, under those circumstances, sleep the day away.

She takes the seat opposite me in the booth, drawing one leg up under her to sit on. She wears oversized comfortable bottoms and a baggy sweatshirt, both a pale grey. Her hair is piled up in a messy bun. It suits the pretty face underneath, which is free of makeup.

'You look different.' There's that hint of a smile again. Her ears, now I can see them, have multiple piercings. 'What can I get you?'

'I like to give my face a break on Sundays. I'd love a coffee please, black, no sugar.'

'Anything to eat?'

'No, I don't want to put you out.'

'It's fine,' I reassure her. 'I'm going to get something.'

'Oh all right, a toasted and buttered teacake, please.'

'Sounds good, I'll make that two,' I say, and go to place the order. As I return to our table, I realise how much less threatening I find her this morning, without the warpaint. I may be the more adult one of the two of us, but I have to admit that I'd previously found her intimidating. Maybe that's what she wants, to be unapproachable. Perhaps she doesn't realise how she comes across when fully Goth.

When I get back, I tell her of my surprise at her wanting to meet so early. Didn't she want to sleep in after working last night?

'In an ideal world, yes. But I have a lot of schoolwork to do for my A Levels and I can't keep on top of it if I lose a day.'

'I admire your dedication. What subjects are you taking?'

'Fine art, photography and English literature. I'm planning on studying fine art at uni.'

'Sounds like you have a plan,' I say as the teacakes arrive. 'My best friend is an artist.'

'Cool. What medium?'

'He paints and sculpts, mostly horses, but sometimes other animals. His name's Harry O'Connor. Maybe you've heard of him?'

'Oh, yes, I've seen an exhibition of his in town. I love his work in wood.' I smile. That's my favourite too, and I feel proud on Harry's behalf. 'But I don't think you met me here to talk about art,' I reply, and she takes a bite from her teacake. I've already started mine so clear my mouth before speaking.

'This is what I know, Unity. Someone killed my friends, and I don't think it was Charlie. I think Jenny is the key, though. That's where it started, the attack. I think you were friends with her and you both have that link with Liberation. That's pretty much all I've got.'

'We weren't friends. Not like proper friends.' That takes me by surprise.

'Oh.' I'd jumped to that assumption. I think for a second and press on, 'But you know something, Unity. I know you do.' She tips her head from side to side as she finishes her teacake.

150

'This is what it was. I only came to this school for its sixth form, so although we were at the same school, we hadn't grown up together through it. We did completely different subjects and had no friends in common.'

'Go on.'

'The first time Jenny ever spoke to me was when she saw me behind the bar at Liberation. It was late, and she appeared from one playroom. I hadn't seen her earlier in the evening, but she was pumped with it all.'

'Did you see anyone with her?'

'No. It was like she was walking out with a group of other people, then came over. She was all, like, this is so cool, and I had no idea you worked here.' Unity puts on a voice that is nothing like Jenny's, but never mind. I get the gist.

'What happened next?'

'She started seeking me out at school, wanting to talk about Liberation and what went on there, but we had completely different experiences of it. I mean, I've never, well, you know, done any of the stuff there. It was purely a job to me. A bar job. But she didn't want to talk to her actual friends about it, thought they wouldn't understand. So she wanted to talk to me about what went off on the other side of those doors.'

'Did she make you uncomfortable?'

'Kind of. I thought she was pretty young to be getting into all that. The people there are generally older, but you know,' and she grins at me sheepishly, 'I'm only human, so I was sort of intrigued too.' Understandable. I'd had similar thoughts since my brief visit.

'Did you see who she was there with?'

'No, you know what the bar's like. You can barely see beyond the first row of faces. But she told me at school that he was older and her parents wouldn't approve. I could tell she loved confiding in me.'

'Did she tell you anything else?'

'I heard all about Charlie and saw him around at school. Felt sorry for him, actually.'

'Why?'

'He thought they were in some special and exclusive relationship. Thought she went on the pill for him and she led him on, told him he didn't need any other contraception. That he was "The One",' and she uses air quotes.

'She used him?'

'Oh, yes. She told me how sweet he was and what perfect cover he provided for her other activities, as she liked to call them. I kind of got the impression...' She hesitates, looks awkward, but I don't want her to stop now. I want to hear it all, so I push on.

'About what?'

'That she was sleeping around? There was the older guy she bragged about, but it wouldn't surprise me if there were others, too. There certainly were at the club, she told me as much.' I sit back in my seat. She puts out a hand to me. 'I'm sorry, perhaps I shouldn't have said all that, but I didn't think she was being fair to Charlie. She could have been spreading anything around, but because he didn't know the truth, he wasn't taking any precautions to protect himself.'

'No,' I shake my head at her concern, 'that was exactly what I needed to know. It's a shock though when you've known someone all their life and you find out you didn't know them at all.' I take a minute to finish my coffee, and get on to the part I don't think she's going to like. 'You should tell the police all of this.' I doubt they've found out about this part of Jenny's life, not if her friends didn't know about it.

'They won't be interested. They've got their man.'

'Yes, but it's the wrong man. I'm sure of it. You've already said you feel sorry for Charlie. Don't let him stay in prison for something he didn't do.' I hesitate, as having Unity come forward could cause more trouble for Harry. However, I'm certain, even though he was involved with Jenny, he isn't a murderer. The police need to be looking further afield, or perhaps revisiting Gary or Eric, and knowing Jenny frequented this club might widen their net. 'Look,' I say as I rifle in my bag for the card DI Pattison gave me. I'd stored his details in my phone, so hand the card over to Unity. 'Call DI Pattison, or DS Barker. Tell them you have some information, and tell them what you've told me. It might at least cast some doubt on Charlie's involvement.'

She looks at the card. 'Okay. I will.'

'Do you want me to come with you?'

'No, I'll be okay. But I won't be able to see them until later in the week. I've got too much on over the next couple of days.'

'That's fine, whenever is better than never. Will you let me know once you've been in?'

'If you like,' she says, and we swap numbers.

'Thanks, Unity, I appreciate you meeting with me.'

'You're welcome.' She gets up to go. 'Maybe I'll see you at the club again one night,' and she laughs.

'Yeah, maybe you will, but I think Hell might have to freeze over first.'

153

17: Betrayal.

While I work the following morning, I think about how Seb was with me last night. His behaviour was strange enough to have me dwelling on it today, although it had started off perfectly fine. He had come back late afternoon and got on with preparing our dinner, a full roast. Beef, Yorkshires, the lot. I love it when he spoils me.

True to his word, he opened a bottle of wine and had even run a bath for me so I could have a soak while he finished the cooking.

When I came back downstairs, rosy pink and relaxed, he'd already set the table and now poured the wine. He served up while I counted my blessings.

When he eventually sat, he raised his glass, clinking it against mine. 'Here's to our future family.'

'To our future family,' I repeated, hoping this would be the year my hopes came to fruition. 'How was your father?'

'Not too bad, considering. A bit shaken, of course, and he'll be sore for a few days, but he was lucky not to break anything.'

'It surprised me you stayed over. I know you prefer not to.'

He always moans and groans about having to sleep there as the house is massive, draughty and freezing. At some points during the year it's bearable, but in January, no. His parents keep three rooms heated, the kitchen, living room and their bedroom.

'It was awful. The sheets on my bed were damp and at breakfast I found mouse droppings in the butter. I don't know how they can live like that.' It sounded miserable and part of me was thankful he hadn't taken me up on my offer to go with him.

Our house is a large stone farmhouse. The ceilings are high, the rooms big. It stretches to three floors with steep stairs and balconied landings. It's not fancy, but we have carried out work to make it warm and cosy. Having to stay at his parents' place after the comforts of here is a jump. Although I can't quite understand why they don't sell up and buy something smaller and more comfortable.

'What about your mother? Is she coping all right?'

'She was the reason I stayed, actually, to give her a bit of a break. Plus, it gave me the opportunity to check the house over for potential hazards, seeing as we've had one fall, and got away with no serious injury.'

'What do you mean, like extra grab rails?'

'Yes, I made them walk around the house and noted where they were struggling. Both have become less mobile quite quickly. I'm going to research what's needed, buy the necessary and go back in a few weeks' time to fit it all.' I considered whether I should say anything as I take my next mouthful. The beef was excellent. Seb may have many talents but he's not exactly a natural with DIY, however I bit my tongue from suggesting that it might be a better idea to have the supplies delivered to his parents' place and arrange for a local handyperson to fit them. As I didn't want to dampen his enthusiasm; I changed the subject instead.

'How did the meetup with Toby go?'

'Excellently. I can't believe how much he's changed.'

'You always say that, and it's less than a month ago that you last saw him.'

'It's true. They grow up so quickly.' He reaches out and places his hand over mine, and stroked it with his thumb. 'I can't wait for us to have our own baby, Laura, then you'll see exactly

155

what I mean.' I smiled back at him, loving his enthusiasm. 'I am going to be completely hands on and present for all the changes this time.'

'That's great to hear. I didn't expect you to want to be as involved as all that, considering you've already been through it once.'

'I didn't get the chance to do any of it with Toby. That bitch Tilly was such a control freak. Everything I did was wrong, and she never stopped going on at me until I'd lost all confidence in doing anything with him.'

It was my turn to reach out to him this time. 'That's sad. What a horrible thing to do. You had as much right to be involved as she did.'

'I'm glad you see it that way. Let's hope I make a better job of it this time,' he smiles brightly, though I can sense the underlying bitterness at the lost opportunity.

'I will make sure you get to do everything you want with our baby. In fact, I am thrilled you want to be so involved as I will still have a yard to run, so having a hands-on dad around will be terrific.' We hadn't opened up to each other as much about the baby before and it was such a positive conversation I allowed myself to feel the tiniest bubble of excitement rise up inside at the thought of our future family life together.

Seb refilled our glasses. I'd nearly finished eating. 'That's the best meal I've had in a while. It was delicious.'

'Thank you. I do like to do a roast, as you know.' It is his speciality. He took another potato, then asked, 'What have you been up to over the weekend?'

It was always going to be a standard weekend for me, so he usually wouldn't bother asking. 'Nothing out of the ordinary. Everything has ticked over in the yard. No one fell off, there were no injuries, so all in all, it was a calm weekend.' I didn't feel the need to say anything about my trip to Liberation, or my subsequent meeting with Unity. If I'd told him about how I'd tracked her down, I'd have had to tell him about going to the sex club and, as we are equally matched in that side of life, I didn't think he'd appreciate me going there alone. In fact, I think he'd have been shocked, and I didn't need him going on, especially as he'd initially dismissed Unity's interest in Number 9. While I don't enjoy withholding information from my husband, sometimes it's necessary, especially when you're sharing a lovely meal and hoping for a bit of romance in the bedroom for afters.

That's the problem with my early nights. Seb and I don't have the same bedtime, which is hardly conducive to the baby-making process, so we often go to bed early to do what comes naturally. Afterwards he'll wander off downstairs to watch some television while I pop a pill and know nothing more until morning.

'You didn't go out on Saturday night?'

I felt a flush come to my cheeks as I answered, 'No.' If he noticed, he said nothing. Probably thought it was the wine.

'Oh, I thought you might meet up with a friend as I was away for the night.' Leaving aside the small matter that my closest friend had recently been murdered and my other one was currently abroad, it wasn't the sort of thing I did that often, anyway.

'No, you know a quiet night in is more my style.'

He tilted his head as if appraising me. 'I know, but do you never get bored doing the same thing day in and day out? I know you have the tie of the horses, but don't you ever want to do something different?'

'No, I don't, actually. I'm perfectly happy with my life,' I said, but his question unsettled me. Perhaps it's his way of telling me he's bored with this steady life of ours. 'How about you? With these questions you're asking, perhaps you're not as content as I am.'

'No, no,' he'd said. 'I'm perfectly happy, but of course, I have my days in London, so I see other people and eat out whenever I want.' Perhaps we should make more of an effort to go out around here. The Red Calf has a varied menu, and the food is good, so perhaps we could go there more often or try out some other places in local villages, even going into town if we could find somewhere recommended. As he was the chief cook now, it would give him the night off, too. Date nights, that was it. We should have date nights.

'Perhaps we should go out around here more often?' I suggested.

'Absolutely, if you want to. I enjoy trying new places, but I'm okay with things as they are, too.' He drained his glass before he added, 'So what have you been up to while I was away?'

I nearly made a joke about his advancing years and dementia creeping in as he was repeating himself, but because of his sensitivity on the subject, didn't.

It's left me thinking this morning, though.

What did he think I'd been up to?

Anyway, the sex after was great. Seb is always sensitive and thoughtful about my needs in bed. That side of our relationship maybe misses the passion and fireworks I had with Matt, but that was different. We were young, our lives lived at a furious pace, our sex life as athletic. Things are different now, more considered, and, let's face it, we are older, so I'm sure you can't expect the same level of excitement to be maintained. Seb's always satisfied too, says as much actually. So everything is fine on that front. Now if I could get pregnant, that would be the icing.

I'm not sure how long to leave it before seeking medical help, but I think we've probably been trying for long enough. Maybe I should make an appointment with my doctor. However, it's hard to think about life moving on so soon after the tragedy, so I resolve to consider it again in a few weeks. Maybe by then I won't need to bother.

I try to clear my mind by concentrating on the work in hand, but it's difficult because the whole situation following the murders is deeply unsettling for all, the atmosphere pervading the village one of suspicion and dread. Life around the stables is understandably subdued, and it occurred to me the other day what was missing. Harry's whistle. Since I found the bodies that's stopped and I'd been so used to hearing it in the background, the yard a darker place without it. But it's not the only change, there's much more beyond that. More often than not, there's plenty of activity, people in and out, deliveries, conversation, laughter. Now a sadness hangs over the stables, over the entire village. Conversations in hushed tones. Any joy muted for fear of giving offence. With someone in prison for the crime, rightly or wrongly, the initial fear some had has gone and in its place people mourn for the loss a family that was central to the whole community.

As each day passes, I've noticed my mind is less consumed by the deaths, but guilt taints any relief this brings because my friends are slipping away too quickly.

I go about my work and today there's little interaction with anyone else. Harry and Pip are each doing their own thing. We had an early conversation about who is riding out which horses and what teaching Pip has on, and ever since it's as if we've each disappeared into our own little worlds to get on with it.

I have a guilty conscience when I see Harry and consider telling him about Unity and the conversation we'd had with her disclosure of the older man in Jenny's life, to give him the heads up on what she is going to do this week, but I don't. The police have questioned him twice already. They must have satisfied themselves of his innocence by now. Plus, I know he is blameless and, thus convinced, I don't say a word. After all, what difference would it make if I did?

I keep harking back to the latest conversation I had with Pattison, though. Why didn't Harry tell me it was Jenny who hadn't turned up to work New Year's Eve? Why didn't he call her to see if everything was all right?

Also in the back of my mind all day is the concern that Unity may not follow through and contact the police, and I keep checking my phone to make sure I haven't missed a message from her.

I don't hear until late afternoon. She's spoken to Barker, and he's arranged for her to come in on Thursday morning, as she has a late start at school that day. I feel myself relax at the news. She hasn't reneged on her promise, and I don't have to go through the rigmarole of hunting her down again.

The days move at a glacial pace with each hour dragging, and I have to force myself to stop checking the time. I'm tempted to call Pattison myself and put him in the picture, basically willing to do anything to enable the release of Charlie as early as possible. But I don't because first, after my last conversation with him at the family gathering, I feel I've lost any credibility I may have had and, second, I think it will weaken what Unity has to say. It may sound like we've colluded, whereas fresh information from a new witness will be better received than coming second-hand from me. I sincerely believe this evidence will cast enough doubt to make Charlie's release a real possibility. Because I don't think the police are even aware of Jenny's connection with Liberation. No one knew about it apart from Unity and I guess the people she was cavorting there with, and they are hardly likely to come forward, so it must raise several new avenues of investigation and potentially many more suspects to interview. Who else might Jenny have met at Liberation? Could the murderer be among them? Jenny unwittingly bringing a killer into the family home. The thought makes me shudder.

I check in a couple of times with Sally and have to resist telling her what's going on, as I don't want to raise false hope. Although I've already decided to call and tell Steve once Unity has been in. He can put the pressure on for Charlie's potential release from that angle.

There has been some sort of police presence in the village throughout January. At first, they naturally concentrated it on Number 9, the forensic team taking several days to complete their investigations. The search, although hampered by the short days at this time of year, widened from there. I've seen officers conducting a fingertip search of the spacious garden of Number 9. They've also been through my paddocks, as I was told they provided the killer with a means of escape. They've thoroughly searched the hedges and ditches too. There have been door-to-door enquiries, many interviews carried out, and statements taken. A few days ago, the police started searching the drains throughout the village. I pass them while out on a lovely mare,

Kate, who snorts with suspicion at their antics as she sidles past. The drain covers are up as they delve into the contents. They never get as far as examining the one outside the stables, though. The missing knife, the suspected murder weapon, is discovered down the drain outside the manor house next door. Where Harry lives.

Harry doesn't react at the news when one of the livery owners announces it on her arrival. He merely pushes his barrow to the next stable and continues mucking out.

On Thursday morning, I send Unity a good luck message and ask her to let me know how it went. Late morning, I get a thumb up sign on a text which I take to mean job done, although frankly I would have liked more detail.

I'm frustrated I don't know more about what is going on at the police station, which only adds to the feeling of impotence I've suffered throughout. I'd love to have been be privy to the post-mortem reports and the forensics. The clues the police were getting. Maybe I'm nosy, or maybe it's because it's so close to home, but I'm curious as to what information they have been acting on. Like now. Are they taking Unity's statement seriously or, as she thinks, have they dismissed it? What questions might it raise in their minds? What, if anything, are they now following up on? And what of the murder weapon? Has that provided any further clues? So many questions. Endless possible answers. My mind switches rapidly from one to another, an exhausting cycle I know is pointless but cannot stop.

During afternoon stables I get the call. Charlie has been released and Sally sobs her relief into the phone. I yell the news across the yard, gratified to hear a cheer go up.

Harry suggests a trip to the pub for their regular Fish and Chip Night by way of a small celebration. We all decide to go, Seb and Pip too. It's a relief to be out, and the pub is busy, the Fish and Chip Night always a popular one.

Once seated, we raise a discreet glass to Charlie because we know his release will not be universally popular, the fear levels potentially rising among some in the population again.

Pattison and Barker arrive as we're eating. I see them appear in the doorway, directly behind where Harry sits. My knife and fork poise over my plate as my throat dries. There's a ripple effect as other patrons notice their presence. The noise in the bar drops by degrees. Harry clocks my stillness, makes eye contact, and I indicate to the reason with the barest lift of my chin. He puts down his cutlery, turning in his seat to check out the new arrivals. As if they were waiting for this moment, they cross to our table. A hush falls.

I stand. 'Seriously!'

Pattison doesn't respond, simply looks from me to Harry. 'Harry O'Connor, I am arresting you for the murders of John, Jan, Jenny and Judy Jackson. You do not have to say anything. But, it may harm your defence if you do not mention when questioned something which you later rely on in court. Anything you say may be given in evidence.'

'I can't believe you've still looked no further than Harry.' Pattison turns his gaze on me.

'The connection you provided us with via Unity has proved hugely informative. Thank you, Laura. We have all we need to take Harry in for further questioning.'

I look at Harry in horror. His expression is one of defeat and disappointment in me. My betrayal is clear to see.

'I'm so sorry, Harry. I never meant…' He holds a hand up to stop me, shakes his head.

'I'll be back before you know it. Don't worry.' Ashen-faced, he doesn't look as confident as his words.

He's led outside, put into the back of a police car and driven away. We're left stunned. *Don't worry? Like we're going to do anything else.* My stomach roils and I wish I hadn't eaten.

I've done all I can to free Charlie, only to have the weight of guilt swing firmly back onto Harry. I can't bear to look at Pip, can only imagine the accusation written across her face. Because only one question runs on repeat through my mind. What have I done?

18: The Mrs Percivals: Twice the Delight.

Seb doesn't make an issue over Unity. Probably because he can see the state I'm in. I tell him I'd tracked her down at school and encouraged her to go to the police. She'd known Jenny was seeing an older man, which put Harry right back in the frame. The police are apparently unable to see beyond him, the only silver lining being that it cast enough doubt on the evidence for holding Charlie any longer.

Alone, though, I can't help but dwell on the fact Pattison had said they had all they needed to take Harry back in from the information Unity had provided. As much as I protested his innocence, I assumed that meant that he was Jenny's older man and they must have proven this from the member records held by Liberation. It shouldn't have surprised me, of course. He'd told me what Jenny was into, but because of his reticence in telling me, I'd assumed he wasn't. It now appears I was wrong. Clearly he was part of her scene at Liberation, and by pushing Unity to go to the police, I'd dumped him right in it.

I am thankful I have a pill to take tonight, otherwise I don't think I'd have slept a wink.

Seb is due to go to London the next day, Friday. He takes the early train so comes into the kitchen while I'm contemplating having my breakfast, wondering if it will stay down if I do. He's smartly dressed and ready to leave, but peers at me with concern.

'You don't look well, Laura.'

'Oh, I'm fine,' I say, and wave away his concern. 'I'm anxious, that's all, for Harry.'

'Of course, I understand. Shall I stay here with you?'

'That's thoughtful, but no. There's nothing you can do, so you should go to work.'

'Okay,' he says as he kisses me on the cheek, 'I'll try not to be late but I have a dinner to attend and you know how they can drag on.'

'It's no problem. I'll see you when I see you, which will be tomorrow,' and we both smile at our little 'in' joke.

He leaves and I go out into the dark to make a start on the day. I'm keen to get going as I want to free up some time later for a project I need to tackle.

The reason I was eager for Seb to go to work is that I rarely get the house to myself and don't know when I next will. Therefore, despite my worries about Harry I have to make the most of Seb's absence because his birthday is at the end of February and, having come up with the idea of what to do to celebrate it, I realise I can't put off the calls I need to make to his family any longer.

I decide to tackle the one I think will be easiest first. His parents. Seb tells me they live in some dilapidated pile and when we met they came across as landed gentry, albeit in rather weathered form because of having had to sell off some assets in the past, which has left them with a lack of income. Seb tells me the place is crumbling around their ears but they refuse to leave, being determined the place will 'see them out' a phrase his mother even used in front of me.

It is she who answers with a forceful, 'Caroline Percival.' I'm inexplicably nervous.

'Oh, good afternoon, Caroline. It's Laura here.'

'Laura? I don't know any Laura.'

'Er, I'm Seb's wife?' I say, making it sound like I'm even questioning the fact myself.

166

'Oh. Yes, of course. Laura. I was miles away. How can I help you?' I'm not sure if it's my imagination, but as soon as she realises who it is, I detect an added edge to the ice in her voice.

'Well, Seb is going to be fifty in a few weeks.'

'I'm perfectly well aware of that, thank you.' *She's his mother*, I tell myself, *don't say unnecessary things*. As she's clearly not one for small talk, I try to be succinct, as she already sounds annoyed with me. Not sure why.

'I was thinking I'd like to plan a small surprise gathering for him.' There's silence from the other end, so I plough on. 'Only the family, you and his da… er, father, hopefully Toby.'

'Where were you thinking?' I'd forgotten how abrupt she could be.

'At that restaurant we met at before, maybe?' I pause, seeking some kind of sign as to whether or not this suggestion is meeting with her approval, but inwardly cursing myself for sounding so apologetic.

'I suppose that could work,' she says begrudgingly. 'It would be good to see Toby again, and of course Sebastian, as we haven't seen him since before Christmas. I don't know what he finds so fascinating about life in that dreary little village of yours that keeps him from visiting.'

Silence.

From my end this time.

Blood drains from my head.

I realise I can hear a voice. It gets louder.

'Hello… hello? Are you still there?'

I come to. 'I'm sorry, poor connection.' My voice is weak and distant.

She tuts. 'Look, text me the details, will you?' My invitation clearly an irritation sent to inconvenience her day. The call ends. The kitchen chair catches my fall.

They haven't seen Seb since before Christmas.

What about last weekend? His father's fall? If he wasn't with them, then where was he?

I almost call him to demand an immediate answer. But don't. I let her words sit with me for a while. I'd prefer to speak to him face to face anyway, so I can see his reaction. Read his expression. It's so much harder to hide in person than when you're on the phone. And of course, there might be a simple explanation. Yes, I decide, that'll be it. A simple explanation. I say this out loud to my empty kitchen, as if that might sound more convincing. Scout has come through from the utility room and I lean forward in my seat to pet her for a few moments until I settle on what to do next. One thing I do know. If there does turn out to be a simple explanation, I'll kick myself for wasting this day by not calling Tilly.

It had been hard enough to get hold of her number, after all. One day, Seb had left his phone on the table when he'd gone to answer the door. I'd taken the opportunity to seize it before it locked itself and written Tilly's number down on the shopping pad, replacing the phone before he returned.

All I needed to do now was pluck up the courage to use it. In the end, it was a lack of time that drove me to get on and call, as I had to go back out to afternoon stables. That and a certain curiosity to speak to the previous Mrs Percival and find out if she was anywhere near as ghastly as Seb had intimated.

On this point, he had at least told the truth. In fact, if anything he'd understated how absolutely vile she actually was.

My heart pounds as I make the call, and I half hope she won't answer. But she does.

'Tilly Masters,' she barks in my ear. Her voice full of spiky authority and confidence.

'Hello, Tilly. It's Laura here, Seb's wife.' I try to sound equally confident.

'Ohhh, hello, Laura. Fancy hearing from you.' She's posh, draws out her words for effect. But I can tell she's intrigued to get my call. A certain snake-like oiliness in her tone. 'What do you want?' She's equally direct, if not more so than her previous and my current mother-in-law. I explain my idea for a gathering to celebrate the impending birthday and am taken aback by her reaction when I ask if Toby can attend.

'Oh good God, no, that won't do at all. We're perfectly happy with the current arrangement, so I'd prefer to leave it at the status quo if it's all the same to you.' She speaks like that's a done deal, which makes my blood boil.

I'm reminded of Seb's bitterness at not being involved with Toby's upbringing because she undermined him at every turn and can now see exactly how controlling she is.

'No, actually, it's not all the same to me. I think Seb should have the chance to see his son on his birthday. He gets few enough opportunities as it is.' A silence follows while I wait for what I expect to be an explosion. I'm therefore surprised to hear laughter. It's short, a tinkle and little more, but it's there and I can tell she's still smiling when she speaks.

'Oh, Laura, you sweet mousey little thing, you. Sebastian sees plenty of Toby, both at school… and here.'

Here? My mouth dries.

'What do you mean, he sees him here? I mean there.' I'm considerably less confident now, my question guarded.

She laughs again, which only serves to put my back up because it emphasises how much she's enjoying herself. 'Oh. It's his parents he doesn't see, not us. You don't seriously think he'd give me up purely because he married you, do you? How quaint.'

'But you are divorced, aren't you?'

'Oh yes, that went through, ooh…' there's a pause while she does the maths, 'nearly three years ago now, but that's only because we couldn't live together, all those arguments over money and trying to get it out of him. Boring! It wasn't because we wanted to stop bonking each other. And now he's got you for all that tedious day-to-day married stuff. I was glad to be shot of it, to be honest, and I'm totally happy with the fun Sebastian I get to enjoy now.'

'But he has me for all that.' This sounds pathetic, even to me, but I can't bring myself to use the word bonk.

'Believe me, darling, there's absolutely no way you are able to cater to his needs. He's told me as much. Whereas me, I'm supremely capable, so it's a win-win and we both get what we want.' Apparently, I don't factor in the who's getting what they want, as she might as well have gone on to say, "whereas you, little wifey, you get to sit at home and play the fool".

'But we're trying for a baby.' I wish I could bite those words back the moment they are out of my mouth because they prompt a howl of laughter from the other end.

'Oh my God, he's absolutely done you, hasn't he, darling.' She's having to control her laughter. I can hear it. My face burns from the humiliation. 'Let me tell you something,' she says, once she's able to speak again. 'Sebastian had the snip soon after Toby was born. It's not like we didn't love him. Although you have to say that, don't you, otherwise people think you're a beast. It's just, well, we found him a bit of an inconvenience in our lives, that's all. Didn't want any more.' My throat thickens as tears threaten.

I'm lost for words. But that doesn't stop her. 'But you, oh poor you.' Her condescension is unbearable, but there's no sympathy, in fact she's positively gloating, joy clear in every word. 'I'm so sorry to be the bearer of bad tidings but I'm afraid if you're expecting to have a baby with Sebastian you're going to be waiting an awfully long time.' She laughs again and I end the call, too shell-shocked to say anything further.

I realise my face is wet and wipe away the tears, my world crumbling around me.

With too many revelations in far too little time, I can't process them all. I stagger into the living room, collapse on the sofa, and try to make sense of what I've heard. Scout comes and lies on the floor at my side.

He's not been going to see his parents when he says he has; he's been going to see her, the ex. *And he's been sleeping with her!* So much for the animosity he'd said was between them. They could barely speak cordially to each other. That's what he'd told me. *Liar!*

Fury burns through my veins, and I stand again, needing to be on the move. He's taken me for an idiot, and I pace back and forth across the sitting room as I debate what to do. What I want to do is confront him immediately and I'm frustrated by the fact he's not back until later. Much later. Before the call to Tilly, I'd naïvely thought there'd be a simple explanation. There's no chance of that now. Not after Tilly's vicious words. It makes me wonder what else he's been hiding.

All those arguments over money and trying to get it out of him.

The reminder stops me in my tracks.

That's what she'd said. That's why they couldn't live together.

We didn't have money arguments. He paid his share of the bills into our joint account each month in a timely fashion. There had never been so much as a suspicion of an issue with money. Yet you'd think he'd be struggling financially more now that he had his previous family to support too. And boarding school. That didn't come cheap. So, if Tilly couldn't get money out of him back then, with fewer complications, why was he so forthcoming with it now?

I've never seen or had anything to do with his finances. We agreed an amount for him to pay which we were both happy with and that was that. Simple.

While I contemplate this new information, I see the post lying on the front door mat and go to retrieve it. I leaf through the pile. They are all for him, some obviously statements, which piques my interest. Ordinarily, I'd leave everything addressed to him to one side, like a normal person. But since discovering he has already betrayed me today, it takes mere seconds to decide he has lost that privilege. I pick up a knife and start slitting open envelopes.

A bad day gets worse, if that were even possible.

There's a bank statement. He's considerably overdrawn. A credit card. Spent up to the max. Yet, he's never so much as hinted at any money worries.

Last, there's a large packet of papers with a covering letter from a firm of architects based in London. The gist being that they hope they have suitably translated his requirements following their meetings and discussions, and, subject to his approval, they are ready to proceed with applying for outline

172

planning permission. I remove the letter and open the accompanying plans, spreading them across the kitchen table.

I didn't think I could be further surprised today. But Seb has outdone himself. The plans show the extent of The Stables. The house, the buildings, the surrounding land. Although all that is gone. My home, my business obliterated. In their place, and ready for development, a hundred new homes. I realise I'm shaking my head as though in denial. My hand is on my chest, heartbeat racing, and I catch my breath, steady myself against the table. The scale of this audacious move is astounding.

I sit as it hits home how stupid I've been. I blink away tears as there's no time for those now and I take a deep breath to regain control.

He has duped me. Plain and simple. This information, in the form of the plans spread before me, brings a level of awareness that lifts the veil I'd been unaware had been shielding me from the reality of my situation. My entire existence since I met Seb, a lie. How foolish was I to believe I'd found happiness after the devastation of losing Matt? How stupid to think someone could actually love me? Heat comes to my cheeks as I think back to how easy I'd made it for Seb to become part of my life. To how desperate I'd been for someone to love. When all along, all he's been after, all he's ever been after, is my land. It's worth a bit as it is, but get planning permission on it and the value soars. That's why he's hinted at me selling up and retiring. Not for my good, but for his. That was back when he was cajoling me. Trying to get me on board with his plan. Now it looks like he means business and is going to proceed whether or not I'm along for the ride.

I go to his office, mindful of the time as the horses need my attention but on a mission. I go through his drawers. Scout sits in the doorway watching my activity. I never come in here, not since it became Seb's office, so don't know where to start, or what I'm looking for. Astonishingly, he either trusts me or believes himself so clever and me so stupid that I'll not come looking, as the drawers are unlocked. His arrogance staggers me.

Opening the large bottom drawer in his desk, I find the hanging files neatly labelled. I frown at several that have property addresses on them. I didn't know he owned any property. Pulling one out, I open it on the desk. The papers enclosed are actually all to do with the sale of a cottage. But it wasn't, in fact, his. It had belonged to his parents. I can see that from the estate plans. This, a cottage being sold off. I check the other files; they are all the same. Properties that were part of his parents' estate, all being sold. Every six months or so.

I look for bank statements. The ones I find only go back a year but the sale of the last cottage was six months ago and when I check between the bank and the file I can see the large sum of money from the sale deposited into Seb's bank account after the sale went through. It had cleared his debt at the time and left a sizeable sum in the account, but now, only six months later, he's overdrawn again. I collect the statement received today from the kitchen table and look through the transactions, bewildered by how someone can get through so much money in such a short space of time.

Then it becomes clear.

Spending, and on a massive scale. Hotels, restaurants, high-end shops, casinos, bookies, all online, large cash withdrawals for who knows what, the evidence all there in black and white. Money disappearing into a black hole. And me, again the fool, completely unaware.

What about his job? There's no sign of any salary coming into the account. I thought when he went to London it was to work, but now I doubt everything. I search deeper, digging into his files of correspondence. He's meticulous with his paperwork, I'll give him that, and sure enough, eventually I find the letter from his employers sacking him for stealing from them. Dated five years ago.

Why would you keep a letter like that?

I sit back in his office chair and ponder my findings, the hairs rising on my neck when there's no getting away from the realisation that since losing his job, he's been living on the sale of properties that formed part of his parents' estate. He has thereby denied them the rental income that they would have been able to live on comfortably. Instead, he's left them to face an impoverished old age.

What a terrible thing to have done. To his own parents! Why had they stood by him and not said anything?

Probably because one day it was all going to be his anyway, and I know how good he is at talking. I can see how he would have cajoled them into letting him do this, to release early funds for him. Or maybe he told them he was doing it for them, but kept the money. What a shit! They clearly hadn't thought through the consequences of their actions.

I think back to the plans laid out on the kitchen table and give him the benefit of the doubt. Perhaps he is planning on reimbursing them for their loss out of the money he intends to make by developing my property. I shake myself: I'm being too generous. When will I learn? His track record has shown he will merely keep that for himself too. After all, it only needs to keep him going until he can find some other dumb woman to deceive.

Some other dimwit like me.

Because even if I agree to go ahead with the development, once that money is in his hands I know, having got what he wants, he won't hang around.

I shake my head. He'd been so together when I met him. Certainly, he appeared solvent and was generous with his money. Smartly presented too and appeared to be independent, but that's what conmen are good at. Pulling the wool over the eyes of their unwitting victims. Well, he's been caught out this time and I need to confront him with the evidence so he'll realise I'm not the idiot he thinks I am.

When I go back into the kitchen, I check through the credit card statement. Shocked all over again. He spends money like he's some sort of playboy. Pricey restaurants, more gambling sites, expensive hotels. Who's he trying to impress? And I wonder for a moment if it's Tilly, if they are in this together. Or if there's someone else.

I sit back, drained, the yo-yoing emotions taking their toll on my energy levels, but a glance at my watch tells me I'm late for afternoon stables, we're a man down, and while I may be staring down the barrel of a crisis, the horses still need feeding.

It's actually a relief to get back to doing something normal, despite my mind being on overdrive, and as Scout patrols her territory for rats, scooting in and out of the buildings, her hunting instinct on full alert, I press on with my duties. My thoughts are firmly buried deep in everything I've discovered as I try to make sense of it all.

I'm interrupted as Pip calls a hello when she returns from the paddocks where she's taken all the ponies. They act like a herd nowadays and if she leads one out, the others follow on like obedient sheep, which saves several journeys.

'Any news on Harry?' she asks when she appears at Rooster's stable door where I'm adjusting his rugs.

I know she, like me, can't bring herself to believe he's responsible for the killings, but I feel I won't be able to breathe deeply again, and stop feeling guilty, until he's cleared and home. Then I'll have to hope he'll forgive me.

'Nothing yet.' Pip's next question is one I knew would come. I'm only surprised it's taken her this long to ask. Her curiosity finally getting the better of her.

'Can you tell me who Unity is and what she has to do with all this?'

I turn to her as Rooster returns to his hay net. I explain about Unity and the information she had for the police.

'So it seems the police have assumed Harry is the older man and I suspect the evidence proving it is that they've found out he was a member of Liberation.'

'It's not looking good, is it?' Pip sounds resigned.

'That's what worries me, plus of course they actually arrested him this time.' Along with everything else I've uncovered today this continues to weigh heavily on my mind together with the discovery of the murder weapon. Surely the police can see this has been planted. Harry wouldn't be dumb enough to commit murder and drop the weapon down the most convenient drain next to his home. I'd contacted Marny, through Steve, again last night to help Harry, other than that I couldn't think what else I could do.

We need to remain positive, though, and I try to pick Pip's spirits up. 'He didn't do it, Pip. We must continue to believe that.' Her brow puckers with concern as she looks up at me.

'Are you okay, Laura? You look terrible.' I don't doubt that. I'm drawn, nerves tighter than a bow under pressure. But I try to smile.

'It's one damned thing after another, that's all.' It's all building up inside, along with the unease I've sensed since the murders happened, which has never diminished. The feeling I missed something, that I could have done more, even prevented the tragedy if only I'd spoken to Jan and found out what was going on. It's been eating away at me ever since and right now it feels like it will never end.

Pip glances at her watch. 'Look, the first twenty-four hours are nearly up, so they should release Harry in a few hours at the latest, unless…' and her voice trails off.

I continue for her. 'Unless they apply for an extension.' She gives a sigh and looks as fed up as me.

I'd been so relieved when they released Charlie, and now this.

However, I have many other things occupying my mind too and I'm pleased when I finally get to turn off the stable lights and go back to the house because I want plenty of time to prepare for Seb's return.

19: Showdown.

I don't take my sleeping pill. Tonight, I need to stay awake and alert. I have a glass of wine to help me relax, and give me courage. I attempt to eat but find my appetite absent, the contents of my stomach churning at the mere thought of food. Seb is unlikely to be early, so I try to fill the time with something more productive than pacing.

Initially I'm constructive, finding an outlet for my anger in producing everything I need to ensure Seb has no chance to wiggle his way out of this. I lay out the damning evidence, the proof of the debts, the property sales, the plans for The Stables, and it's insurmountable. As I set everything out, I read through it again to be sure of my facts and feel my blood pressure rise as I do. There's going to be no easy way for him to explain any of this, and I'm keen to see how he reacts. I only hope Tilly hasn't tipped him off about our conversation. I'd hate for him to be forewarned.

I try to practise what I'm going to say. How I'm going to lead him along the path of my discoveries, but each time it comes out differently and I know once under pressure I'll not remember a word.

I watch a film, but don't see any of it. I bite my nails, a habit I gave up years ago but one that returns in times of stress. I wonder if Harry is out yet and, if so, why he hasn't been in touch. Is it because he blames me? I worry the period of questioning has been extended instead. I pace and check my watch a lot.

I have another glass of wine.

Shortly after midnight, I hear a car draw up outside. A taxi, which means he's been drinking. A door slams and my heartbeat rises. Much as I've prepared for this, I hate confrontation and wish I didn't have to face it right now. I hear footsteps on the path round the side of the house to the back. I hear a low growl from Scout, which ends once he's inside, and she realises who the intruder is.

He comes through to the kitchen, and closes the door to the utility room quietly behind him. He doesn't suspect a thing because I've left the house as it always is if I've gone to bed. There's a lamp on in the corner, and that's it. I'm in shadow at the table. Sitting perfectly still. He starts when he sees me, which I find pleasing.

'Laura? What are you doing up?'

'I need to talk to you.' My voice is calm. 'Have you had a good day at work?'

'Yes, the usual, you know.' I don't, but that is no longer my concern. He glances at the paperwork spread over the table, unable to see the detail from where he stands. 'Have you had a good day?' he asks tentatively.

'I wouldn't say that, but I have found out a lot of things. Would you like to hear about them?'

'Yes,' he says, because from my tone that's what he thinks I expect of him, not what he wants. 'Though couldn't it wait until morning? I'm knackered.' He's been drinking but isn't drunk, so I see no need to delay.

'No, it can't. I've stayed up for you. The least you can do is listen to me.' His eyebrows rise, but he stays where he is. 'I spoke to your mother today.' His expression changes immediately. He frowns, puzzled.

'Why would you call her?'

'To organise a birthday surprise for you.' His face brightens. But not for long. 'She tells me she hasn't seen you since before Christmas.' I let that sink in but can see straightaway he knows I have caught him out.

'I can explain that—'

'Oh, I bet you can, but for the moment, you don't get the chance.' I hesitate for a moment. 'Next I called Tilly.'

"What! Why would you call her? The evil old bag. I told you I never wanted you to have anything to do with her. You can't believe a word that comes out of her poisonous mouth.' This is the first time his voice has risen and I enjoy watching his discomfort.

'You're quite right, Seb. She is an evil old bag. But I thought I'd put myself through having to talk to her so I could get Toby along to your birthday gathering as a surprise. Can you guess what she told me?'

He shakes his head. 'I've no idea. Everything she says is lies,' he adds, as though getting in a pre-emptive strike. I rise from my seat, and walk round to the other side of the table so I'm closer to him, all the better to see that reaction.

'She told me you two were still fucking.' I see him wince. He hates me to use foul language. 'She told me you'd never stopped and that you couldn't get enough of her. She told me that whenever you were supposed to be with your parents, you were with her.' He opens and closes his mouth like a gasping carp and doesn't know how to respond. I move a step closer. 'And do you know what else she told me?' It's a rhetorical question so I carry on. 'She told me you'd had the snip after you had Toby. Something else you not only failed to tell me, but actively led me on about by pretending we were trying for a baby. You. Lying. Shit.' My gritted teeth cause my jaw to ache.

'It's all lies.'

'That's what you're going with, is it? You see, Seb, I don't believe you. Because look what else I've uncovered,' and I gesticulate towards the papers on the table. 'Debt, Seb. Piles and piles of it.'

'You've been through my papers…' he sees the plans, his eyes widen, 'you've opened my post! That, Laura, is a gross invasion of my privacy.' Fury emanates from him as he moves towards the table to see what I have. Closer now, he leans in, his finger right in my face, and I flinch as he stabs his words home. 'You had no right to do this.'

'I had every right. You're trying to develop my home for housing. How dare you tell me I have no right. You are not the man I thought you were. You're a thieving, conniving conman, willing to rip off his own parents for money.'

'That's not true!'

'You've sold their assets out from under them and left them destitute. All to pay for your extravagant lifestyle… and, you don't even have a job.' I lean towards him, pushing one of the property files into his chest. 'It stops here.' He sneers.

'You think so, do you? You don't know the half of it.'

'What, you mean there's more? Why doesn't that surprise me? *You* are a disgrace, Seb, and when Toby finds out he will be ashamed to have you as his father.' He stares at me, frozen by my words. My low blow. But he's earned every word. As he contemplates his next move, his lips twist into a sneer. An expression I've never seen on him before, and a trickle of fear slithers down my spine. Too far. I've gone too far. Then, as though a switch has been thrown, he abruptly turns and crosses the kitchen, reaching to take the pot of my sleeping pills out of the cupboard. 'What are you doing?'

'You need to take one of these.'

'No, I don't, not yet, Seb. We need to deal with this. Then you can leave.'

'I'm going nowhere. And stop calling me Seb. My name's Sebastian.'

'I've always called you Seb. You never said you didn't like it.'

'I'm saying it now.'

'In fact, you told me you liked me shortening it. You told me that's what made me special.'

'Special? I've despised you for it, every single time, because you're so fucking lazy you can't even be bothered to call me by my proper name.'

I bristle at the accusation. Lazy is the last thing I am.

'All right, Sebastian,' and I emphasise each syllable. 'I know what you are, a cheat and a liar, and I want you out of my house and life.'

'That won't work for me, sweetheart. You have no idea who you're dealing with, while I've known exactly what you've been up to.' I look at the papers again, confused. How could he have known I'd found out about this? He'd been out all day.

'I've watched you scrabbling around, doing your pathetic Miss Marple bit.' He waves his phone at me. 'I know you've been to the school and to Liberation.' He scoffs. 'That must have been an eye-opener. Talk about being out of place.' He looks me up and down like I'm dirt.

'You've been, what? Tracking me?' I clench my fists. 'How?'

'Via your phone.' He sneers, like it's so obvious. 'It tells me exactly where you are. For example,' and as if about to confide he leans towards me, his lips close to my ear as he whispers, 'I

183

knew the moment you found the bodies.' I lurch away from him, wide-eyed.

Our conversation on how they'd died leaps to mind.

Would I have heard a gunshot?

I'm not sure you would. Not with those sleeping tablets you take.

That's what he'd said.

His assumption they'd died at night.

In bed.

Yet I hadn't told him that's where I found them.

There's a long pause. Our eyes locked on each other.

My unease at what I'd missed… gone.

As the penny drops.

Only way, way too late.

I stare at him in horror. Try to swallow, not sure I can get the next words out.

'You knew they were dead.' My voice hoarse.

'Yes, I did and I can't tell you how much I've been wanting to talk to you about them.'

'You?' Disbelief still edges my voice. He smiles in a way that curdles the contents of my stomach. I back away.

'Not so fast,' he says, and seizes my wrist, holding it so tight I fear my bones might snap. He pulls me to him. 'Tell me what she looked like.' There's a glint in his eyes I don't care for.

'Who?'

'Jenny, of course.'

'She looked peaceful.' He nods, contrition written across his face.

'I didn't mean for her to die.' Fear weakens my limbs. *Oh my God, he's actually admitted it.* Up until this moment, up until this exact point, I thought this was going to be a row about his

184

cheating and lies. I thought he'd leave tonight, we'd break up in time, divorce and that would be that... but this... this is something else entirely.

My breath catches in my throat; as an icy fist closes around my heart.

Suddenly, I'm acutely conscious of the danger I'm in.

I need to keep him talking until help arrives. Not that I imagine any is coming, but it's all I have to work with. Time.

'You were having an affair with her?' The thought makes me want to retch. His smile is wistful, like he's remembering sweet summer picnics on the lawn. He relaxes his grip slightly, increases the distance between us.

'Something like that. You can imagine my surprise when I first saw her in Liberation. It must have been fate that threw us together, as it was the only time I'd ever been to the local branch. My membership is in London. My first thought was that this would shake up those boring old parents of hers, had they known where she was. Then she started talking to me, flirting actually, a bit of fresh young blood, exactly what I was looking for.' He preens at this memory, and I can see how it would have puffed up his flagging ego.

The older man.

Not Harry. Or Eric. Or Gary.

Him.

Bile rises up my throat, I swallow it back.

'We went to a playroom. And fucked over and over. Quite the spectacle we made; I can tell you. People watched, Laura. Imagine that. Being watched. She was magnificent, absolutely magnificent. We drew a crowd, she was that brilliant, and she loved it, every minute. The voyeurism turned her on you see, me too, come to that.' I realise I'm listening to this open-

185

mouthed and close it quickly, not wanting him to see the effect his words are having. His hand still clasps my wrist tight enough that there's no escaping it. But I need to keep him talking while I work out what to do so I prompt him because we're in this far and now I want to know it all.

'Then what happened?'

'We carried on seeing each other outside the club. All terribly hush hush though.' He grins like it's all a game, that wild glint back in his eye, and for the first time since I met him, I question his sanity. 'She'd call me if she had the house to herself. Dared me to fuck her in the garden one day, Laura. Not in the comfort of her own bed, but alfresco. Shortly after that, the role play started.'

'Role play?' I ask, as my voice cracks. He looks at me and shakes his head like he despairs of me.

'You are so fucking naïve. Jenny liked me to pretend to break into the house at night and come to find her.' The pieces of the puzzle, like a jigsaw, fall into place. 'She liked me to pin her down. She enjoyed being raped.'

'No one enjoys being raped,' I dare to say. He grits his teeth, leans in close.

'She did, believe me. She couldn't get enough of it.'

'So what went wrong?' He looks away as though the truth of his actions has finally hit home.

'She called one night and told me to come round.'

'While her parents and Judy were in the house?' I can't quite believe that.

'It wasn't the first time. She loved it, said it added to the danger.' I find myself agreeing as if that's totally understandable and realise, once again, how little I knew Jenny.

186

'I did as she wanted. I never actually broke in of course but creeping into that house in the dead of night certainly got the old ticker thumping I can tell you,' I'm not sure if he is expecting me to applaud his daring exploits or not but the matter-of-fact way he's telling me all this is extraordinary. It's pouring out of him and he's relishing every moment, like he's been waiting for the opportunity to show off. 'I'd wear latex gloves, of course, to add to the drama, and this time I picked up a knife that was on the side in the kitchen. Thought that would spice things up and my God did it.' I try to swallow but find it difficult. 'She was rampant that night, I tell you, bloody gagging for it she was, and she wanted me to choke her.' He looks at me, a gleam in his eye. 'Can you see now why fucking you has always been so fucking tedious?'

'You never told me that.'

'Well, I wouldn't, would I. I never told you it was all I could do to get it up for you either, because you stank of horses, but there we go. Fortunately, I had vivid memories of her to inspire me. That's the truth of it. Had to hold it all in, play my part, because I wanted you for something else.' Each sentence he utters cuts me deep. A painful mix of hurt and embarrassment. He goes quiet for a moment, takes a long breath and can't meet my eyes. Downcast, he returns to his last night with Jenny. 'Anyway, I'd had a few drinks. Overdid it. And there she was, dead.'

Forgetting my promise to Pattison, I say, 'What did you do to her to make the marks on her neck?'

'What marks?'

'The darker bruises, like a row of dots around her throat.' He shakes his head like this is the line past which he will not take responsibility for what he's done. A soft smile comes to his lips.

'Ahh. The little minx. That's so like her. I bet she had someone else round before me. It must have been them.' He chuckles, like it's all fun and games, then, remembering I'm there, his smile beatific, he continues, 'I told you she was a dirty girl, didn't I.' He says this like it's a good thing, like he's proud of her. I'm horrified.

'Are you seriously suggesting there was a third man involved with Jenny that day? That she had sex with Charlie? Then before you arrived you're saying there was someone else? How likely is that?'

'It's exactly the sort of game Jenny liked to play.'

I shake my head in disbelief, my voice faint when I ask, 'What happened next?'

'I panicked. Thought I'd better leave. Met Judy coming out of her room and knew I had to shut her up.'

'So you stabbed her?'

'I didn't realise I'd picked up the knife again, had it in my hand when I pushed her back into her room. She shouldn't have come out right at that moment.' *Seriously? He's blaming her?*

'And John and Jan?'

'They knew nothing about it. Snoring away, they were. I slipped into their room and slit their throats as they slept.'

'Why did you have to kill them at all?'

'I was doing them a favour. I didn't want them to have to face the deaths of their daughters. How awful would that have been for them?'

'You were doing them a favour?' I wonder if he can actually hear the things he's saying. If he truly believes them.

'Plus,' and he leans in, conspiratorially, 'one less planning officer around to tip off the wife about my grand plan would have bought me a bit more time to work on you. That can't be a bad thing, can it?' He gives me a cheeky wink.

Ruthless and remorseless. *How haven't I seen this?*

One thing dawns on me. He did all this while I was fast asleep in our bed. So much for me believing I was his alibi. 'Me taking those pills has enabled you to do this.'

'Yes, you must certainly take on some of the blame.' *What? Is he insane?* 'Which reminds me,' and he holds out the sleeping pill he fished out of the pot earlier.

'I'm not taking that.'

'Yes, you are.'

'There's no point. It's not like I'm going to sleep tonight, anyway.'

'Maybe not, but I don't care about that. My only concern is that they find the right amount of the drug in your bloodstream when they find your body.' My heart nearly stops right there.

'You can't.' My voice rises in desperation.

'I can only get my hands on this place if you're dead.'

'Everyone will know it's you.'

'Of course they won't. I'll make an excellent grieving husband.' He is so matter-of-fact that I know he means it and pull away, his grip tightening as I do. Sebastian is far, far stronger and bigger than I am, but I'm not going down without a fight. He pulls me over to the sink, fills a glass with water, and twists me around so he can pin my head to his chest, his hand around my jaw. My pulse racing, I try to remember any self-defence tips I know and stamp with my heel onto the bridge of his foot. He's still wearing shoes and laughs at my feeble effort. He tilts my head back and prises open my jaw, his fingers pinching at the hinge end until the pain causes me to open my mouth and cry out. I hear Scout's bark as he drops the pill in

189

and follows it swiftly by tipping the glass up against my lips. Water splashes everywhere and I have no choice but to swallow, spluttering as I do, coughing as some enters my airway. Once clear, I check round my mouth. There's no pill. It happened too fast for me to do anything to stop swallowing it.

I reach for a plate drying on the side, swinging it round to smash him over the head, 'Argh!' he cries, as shards of china skitter across the floor. 'You bitch!' he yells as he spins me round to face him once more. Blood trickles from out of his hairline. But I've done nothing to slow him down. Scout is barking repeatedly from behind the closed door now. She knows something's wrong. Unfortunately, the stone walls are thick and we're too far from any other property for it to alert anyone. No point in me screaming, for the same reason. Plus, it's going to take too much energy and I need every ounce of that I have.

'Come on,' he says, and walks purposefully towards the hall, dragging me along. I dig my heels in ineffectually, my slippers gaining little purchase as they slide across the tiles, but when I get to the doorway, I grasp the frame with my free hand. This halts him in his tracks and he turns back to me, a flash of anger in his eye.

He prises my fingers from the doorframe, painfully levering each one away until I don't have the strength to hold on any longer and we're on the move once more. Dragging me to the stairs, I slip and slide along behind him and I seize another opportunity. I take hold of the newel post, halting him again. He's lost patience when he turns back this time, and unwinds my hand from around the post. There are a dozen more before we get to the top, though, and I'm determined to make use of every single one.

190

'Why are we going upstairs?' I demand, my voice breathless as I fight against him freeing me from the post. As I reach for the next one, he kicks my hand away. Pain shoots up my arm.

'How can you expect me to throw you down the stairs if I don't get you up them in the first place?'

'You've thought this through?'

'Of course, it's got to be an accident, otherwise I get nothing.' He releases my hand from the post and to my alarm, lets go of my other hand and wraps his arms around me instead, pinning mine to my body. My back is flat up against his front as he proceeds backwards up the stairs, dragging me with him. I do nothing to help, a dead weight in his arms. The exertion takes its toll on him. I hear his laboured breaths. 'Poor old Laura, they'll say, took a sleeping pill and in her befuddled state fell down the stairs when she went for a wee in the night.' He catches his breath. 'I'll naturally be distraught at finding your cold dead body in the morning. Your neck broken.'

I wonder how long he's been planning this. He might not have expected to be doing it tonight, but he's had it all worked out. The thought chills me.

I can do nothing other than flail my lower arms around ineffectively. My only hope now is that the fall doesn't kill me. Unlikely, as it's down steep wooden stairs onto a stone floor, and I doubt the minor matter of me still being alive afterwards is likely to prevent him from finishing me off.

We're at the top. He stops, and takes a couple of deep breaths as I struggle in his arms. I kick him, aiming for his shins. He grunts, 'Bitch!' but otherwise I have little effect. I try to punch him, awkwardly hitting his thighs, unable to get any power behind the movement, but every effort I make is pointless and with increasing desperation I realise this is it, I'm going to die

191

and there's nothing I can do to save myself. He shifts his hold; I'm lifted clear of the ground. The front door smashes inwards in an explosion of sound. Surprised, I yell, but it's come too late. Without hesitation, I'm launched into the air. Straight over the banister. I scream, flail, and clutch at nothing. Land in a tumble of bodies, my fall broken by someone else's bravery. We hit the ground hard. The wind expelled as I bite my tongue, taste blood. I hear a snap, an expletive as we slide across the floor a couple more feet before finally coming to rest. There are shouts behind us, feet pound up the stairs and all the while the constant bark from Scout in the background. I take a shaky breath, roll off the body I'm partially laid across and, once clear, look back. It's Pattison. He's struggling to sit up, cradling his arm as he does so. Shaking, I gingerly get to my knees, try to help, but he shrugs me away, not wanting to be touched.

Amid the confusion, a quiet moment between us, 'You okay?' he says. It's all I can do to mumble a reply and I'm doing better than him.

'Thank you,' I manage. My voice croaky and I try to swallow.

'You're welcome,' is his gruff response as he turns decidedly green. I remove the plant from the pot at my side, put it next to him like a bin and he throws up into it seconds later.

I look up, see Harry at the door and smile, overwhelmed with relief. He rushes over and slides the last part on his knees, his arms around me in a hug. He looks at Pattison, sees what he's broken, and says, 'I told you to let me in first.'

'Not your job,' Pattison replies through a grimace, clearly in a lot of pain.

'We need to get an ambulance,' I say, wanting Harry to call.

'There's already one outside. They're waiting for the all clear before they can come in.'

Moments later there's a clattering on the stairs to the side of us, a struggle as two officers try to control a handcuffed Sebastian between them. They get to the bottom and turn towards where we remain on the floor.

Pattison looks up at Sebastian, his dislike barely disguised on his face. 'Sebastian Percival, I am arresting you for the murders of John, Jan, Jenny and Judy Jackson and the attempted murder of Laura Percival. You do not have to say anything, but it may harm your defence if you do not mention when questioned something which you later rely on in court. Anything you do say may be given in evidence.' He instructs the officers, 'Take him away.' With that, they turn him around and march him out of the door. Sebastian never so much as glances at me and I wish that is the last time I will ever have to set eyes on him.

I look over at Pattison. 'He told me everything.'

'That should make the process easier.' He attempts a smile, which looks rueful. 'I'm sorry you had to go through this.'

'How were you to know? I lived with him and I didn't.' He shakes his head.

The paramedics enter. One of them checks me over, which they insist on doing even though I'm remarkably unscathed and feel fine. That is, until I try to stand. Dizziness overwhelms as I struggle to breathe, a flush of cold sweeping over me.

'Shock,' says my paramedic to the other.

'Hardly surprising,' is the response. 'You know the drill, but take her into the living room. It's more comfortable.' I'm carried by Harry, and placed on the sofa. He elevates my legs and encourages me to breathe slowly and calmly. Simply seeing

193

his lovely face and knowing he's free helps, but he breathes with me and slowly I start to feel better.

I hear Pattison cry out in pain as the paramedics concentrate on immobilising his arm and soon after, he's led away to be taken to hospital. They come back to check on me, and decide I need to be taken in for observation. I explain I was force-fed a sleeping pill because now I'm quiet, I can feel its relaxing qualities taking over. Harry says he'll come with me.

'No.' I place my hand on his arm. 'I need you to look after Scout and the horses in the morning.' I look at my watch and correct myself. 'In only a few hours.'

'All right, but I'm coming in as soon as morning stables are done, okay?'

'If you insist.'

'I can bring you home with any luck.'

'I want to see Scout before I go.'

'Of course, I'll let her out,' and he leaves my side. Seconds later, Scout bounds into the room, searching me out and making a tremendous fuss of me when she does. Once she knows I'm all right, she scampers off round the house checking out all the intruders.

I leave soon after, stretchered out of the place, which embarrasses me as being over the top, but when I went to stand again, I found I couldn't. Harry and Scout see me off. The police will seal the house, so he'll take her back to his place for what remains of the night. I catch my last glimpse of the pair of them as the doors shut, and stop fighting the urge to close my eyes.

20: Anyone for Cake?

By the next morning, even though every part of my body aches and the bruises incurred from the fall are developing, I'm feeling a lot better and I know it could have been so much worse. I've been able to get out of bed and walk, I've eaten toast and I hope by the time the doctors make their rounds they will sign me off as fit to go home.

Pattison is by my bed. His arm, thankfully, doesn't need operating on, so it's been plastered up and he's stopped by on his way home to get some sleep. He looks shocking. Dark shadows accentuate the bags under his eyes.

I don't expect I look much better.

We have much to discuss and we agree to meet in a couple of days. I'm surprised he will still work the case rather than taking some time off, but he says he won't let it go, not at this stage.

'Are you finally convinced Harry is innocent?' His smile is sheepish, and he holds his one good hand up as if in defence.

'Of course, and I will apologise to him. But, you know, we had valid reasons to arrest him.'

'Did you…?' I'd like him to clarify, but he doesn't.

'As it is, he was the one to put your husband in the frame.'

'Was he?' I'm intrigued.

'He saw them once, together. We took some convincing, but made the connection with Unity's information. Sebastian's name didn't show up on Liberation's database initially because he was only a visitor, but once we delved deeper, well, let's say, luckily for you, we got there in the end.'

'So I have Harry to thank, along with you.'

'Yes,' he looks towards the door as it opens, 'and speak of the devil, here he is.'

Harry carries with him the scent of outside, of hay, horse, and, clearly not having changed since, stables. I feel a pang and a need to get back to where I belong.

'Apologies for any mix-up, Harry, but no hard feelings, eh.' Pattison stands and holds out his good hand to Harry, who shakes it without hesitation.

'No, not now, although I can't say I felt the same twenty-four hours ago.' He takes the seat vacated by Pattison, who tries to brush over his embarrassment as he says goodbye.

Finally, it's the two of us. 'I hear I have you to thank for my rescuers arriving in the nick of time.'

'If they'd listened to me in the first place, they wouldn't have had to rescue you, they'd have made it before all the drama.' He pauses. I see his jaw clench, his frustration barely suppressed.

'Pattison told me you saw them together once.' He looks uncomfortable, but I want to know, so press him further.

'It was last summer. I was out in the back paddock. Do you remember we had a couple of rails down where the ponies had rubbed up against the fence?' I tell him I did. 'I went to fix those early one evening. And there they were in the garden. At least I thought it was him. Difficult to be sure at that distance, so I didn't want to say anything until I absolutely had to.'

Despite Sebastian already having confessed as much to me, I can't help asking, 'What? And they were actually, you know?' and I make a face like I don't want to say the word. Harry merely bows his head by way of confirmation. 'He was having a complete mid-life crisis, wasn't he?' I try to laugh it off but can't quite manage it.

'I think it was something a bit more than that, Laura.' He's not wrong. They will no doubt assess Sebastian, have a label to put on whatever it is.

'Why didn't you tell me you'd seen them together?'

'Would you have listened if I had? I didn't want to cause ructions when I wasn't even certain. So I stayed close instead. See if I spotted anything else.' He's right, I would probably have seen his concern as interference and, in my defender role, not accepted any criticism of my husband graciously. He continues, 'I don't understand how it all blew up last night, though. Did you have suspicions? Did you confront him?'

'Not about Jenny, no. I didn't have an inkling and would have stood up for him to the end. Which shows how stupid I am.'

'You're not stupid. He deceived us all.'

'But I was closest to him. I don't understand how I didn't see it, how I didn't see it all,' and I go on to tell him about the series of discoveries I'd made. His eyes widen with each revelation, and it feels good to get everything off my chest. The process is cathartic. Afterwards, although it's unlikely to be as easy as this, I feel I can now be free to move on.

On our way home, I ask if we can call into the shop. I have a need for carbs, and a selection of their finest pastries, both sweet and savoury, will go down a treat with everyone in the yard.

As we walk in I see my neighbour, Olivia Croxton, balancing a family sized bag of crisps on her already full basket and Dora Smith picking through the potatoes, adding those that make the cut to her bag, and I smile at both. Before any of us can utter a word, Sharon rushes through from the back.

'Good morning! Centre of attention again, I hear,' she exclaims, straightening her tabard. 'The rumours are flying

197

around about you today, Laura. Not that I would pass on a word of them of course, but can I ask, is everything all right at home?' She tilts her head.

'I think you know it isn't, Sharon.' I give her my order and she gets busy filling bags and boxes. Olivia stands behind me, waiting her turn. There's another woman I don't know who appears out of the end of the aisle adding a bottle of wine to the contents of her basket. Her hair is up in one of those enviable messy buns that manage to look both effortless and stylish.

'Oh, that's a shame,' she says, managing to make it sound not at all sympathetic but as though she's still trying to elicit information. 'You would think, wouldn't you, that you'd know the man you're living with?' She shoves a few sausage rolls into a bag using a pair of tongs. 'I mean, I'd know if my Eric was a murderer. That's all I'm saying.'

I smile as sweetly as I can manage, pay and walk away while she carries on talking to my back.

'Maybe it'll be third time lucky, 'cos you've not had much luck with husbands so far, have you?'

I stop. Turn around and return to the counter. Olivia steps out of my way. I lean across and pluck a cream- and jam-filled doughnut from the display. Sharon's eagle eyes follow every move. She leans in. 'That'll be ex—' I squish the cake into her face. There's a gasp behind me and Sharon's eyes widen in surprise as she rears back, the doughnut squashed over nose and mouth, its innards splattered. She tears it away, looks at the mess in her hand, and eyes me with venom. 'Why, you…!' Jam-streaked cream drips from her chin, and, unable to take her fury seriously, I grin. Dora has a hand clamped across her mouth and I hear Harry's laughter as I turn towards him to resume my journey.

'That was…' he says, as we exit the shop.

'… most satisfying,' I finish.

He is still quietly chuckling as we get in the car. 'She's quite insufferable,' I say. 'I've wanted to do that for a while.'

'Shame there weren't more around to witness it.' He laughs again. 'I'm sorry, I shouldn't laugh.'

'You're all right,' I say. 'That's all you can do with that woman. Now, take me home Harry.'

The next morning I'm too sore to ride and Harry insists I take the day off. I have plans I know will keep me busy, so don't argue. The police and forensic officers had packed up and gone by the time I got back from hospital. They've taken a lot of evidence with them. Many of Sebastian's files and paperwork, besides those I'd left out.

Despite being home, however, I'd found it difficult to settle and when I woke this morning, it had come to me. Sebastian's presence is everywhere, and it needs clearing.

I take a roll of black sacks out of a cupboard and go to the top of the house, then work my way down. I go through every room, every cupboard, every drawer, and put anything that has any connection with Sebastian into a sack. As I do so, I consider calling Tilly to tell her what Sebastian has done but I don't, not being able to bear the thought of ever having to speak to that supercilious bitch again but also not wanting her to have the satisfaction of an explanation. Instead, I enjoy clearing his wardrobe, cleansing it of trousers, suits, shirts, ties. There are drawers stacked with jumpers, tee shirts, underwear. All of it I remove, shoving it into bin bags to eradicate every last trace of him.

I pause only once while pulling sweaters from a drawer, when a jangle as something hits the floor makes me peer round the armful I have to see what's dropped. A black leather collar lies on the carpet. The line of chrome studs which adorns the outside push through to become blunted spikes on the inner. I'm sickened once again. Even while confessing, he couldn't admit to this. Couldn't admit to what he'd done to her and passed the blame. I put the offending article in a clear plastic bag. Call Pattison, who says he'll send someone over.

I continue my clearance, astonished at how completely someone can infiltrate your life as the bags pile up. By early afternoon I'm done. I take the last of the sacks out to add to the pile in the car park. I text Tilly, give her twenty-four hours to collect or they're going to the charity shop.

Scout hasn't let me out of her sight since I returned and now, together as always, we head over to the yard, keen to get back to our lives.

THE END

Thank you for reading. If you can leave a few words as a review on Amazon or the retail site of your choice, Goodreads, BookBub or any place of your choosing, then you will feel the warmth of my thanks in the form of a virtual hug. It really does matter as it helps inform other readers whether they should pick up this book or not.

Now follows a teaser of the second novel in the *A Shade Darker* series, *Shape of Revenge.*

2: Mistress of All She Surveyed

To lose one husband may be regarded as a misfortune; to lose two looked like carelessness. This was what occupied Sharon Beesley as she laid out the morning papers. The reminders on every front cover, rubbing it in her face. One week on.

Laura Percival, owner of The Stables and general village do-gooder, centre of attention, once again.

The news was all round the village, of course, the only thing most people could talk about. Not that she'd partake in tittle-tattle, naturally. But it was unsurprising others did, she supposed, given how little happened here most of the time and how small-minded the locals were. Sharon caught her reflection in the shop window, and frowned at her dark roots. She'd have to get the bottle out later, touch those up. She'd been that busy recently, what with the constant flow of reporters and TV crews through the shop, that she'd barely been able to give herself any consideration.

She wouldn't forgive Laura for the cream cake incident either. News of that had spread remarkably quickly, and, much to her discomfort, it appeared the villagers found it entertaining, rather than the assault it clearly was. She'd even caught Eric, her husband, smirking when he first heard of it and had had to remind him of where his loyalties lay.

Sharon glanced out of the shop window to see Manda Babcock waddling into the light cast by the shop. Manda had been a staunch ally, and one who had been sympathetic when Laura had carried out the assault, so Sharon overlooked the fact she was shaped much like a cottage loaf, although with an extra round lump on the top for her head.

'Morning, Sharon. I know you're not properly open yet but I saw you behind the counter and I'm in desperate need of a pint of milk. Hope you don't mind.' Manda breathed heavily despite only living over the road. 'Ooh, I see she's all over the papers again. You'd think they'd have moved on by now, wouldn't you? Shows it's a slow news week.'

'You would, Manda. Although,' and she dropped her voice a notch, '… between you and me, I believe there's a reason they're not letting the story drop.'

'Really? Do tell.' Manda, pint in hand, sidled up to the till, all ears, and Sharon loved nothing more than a captive audience.

'I have been told on good authority, and, Manda, you mustn't breathe a word of this…' Sharon looked at her most seriously as Manda crossed her heart, for all the good that would do in keeping her mouth shut. 'Well,' and Sharon leaned closer, 'there's some talk that Laura wasn't as in the dark about the murders as she's made out.'

'No! Surely not.' The look of disbelief on Manda's face was more than Sharon could have hoped for.

'That's what I've been told.' And she held her hand up as if Manda could take or leave the information. 'There's even talk,' Sharon made a point of looking round the shop, as though checking to make sure they were alone, 'that she might have been involved.' She finished in a whisper barely louder than mouthing the words to impress upon Manda the extreme confidentiality of this information. 'But look, that's strictly between us, all right?'

'Absolutely! I won't say a word.'

'I know I can count on you. Now, the till's not set up yet so have you got the right money?' She reached out a hand. Manda was a frequent visitor because she was as disorganised as they come when it came to groceries, probably because she lived so close and felt she had on-tap access.

'Oh, yes.' Manda, unexpectedly agitated by such disclosures being fed to her at this time in the morning, fiddled in her purse, her pudgy fingers struggling to retrieve the coins needed. This rather tried Sharon's patience but she managed to put on a smile for her most loyal customer. At least until she was on her way out of the door.

Sharon didn't feel the least bit guilty about stirring up any further trouble for Laura as any rumours spread about her didn't appear to matter, she always came out on top. That's what irritated Sharon the most. Laura and her blessed horses held some special place in the village, and could do no wrong, despite the mess they made up Main Street. That was another thing that annoyed her. Although Eric was only too happy to scuttle out to pick up what they'd left behind for his precious roses. It wasn't only Laura. All the horsey toffs irked her, actually. Each one rich enough to pay to have Laura keep their horses for them. It must be nice to be able to afford that sort of hobby.

It hadn't escaped her notice either how the village had rallied around Laura. Sharon had heard them talking in the shop, making plans as to who would deliver food, who had given her a call to check to see she had all she needed.

The problem, as Sharon saw it, was Laura's privilege. The Stables and everything that went with it had been left to her when her mother died, and she took it for granted. She'd not had to work for her business, not like some people. Sharon, for example. She'd had to graft for her place in the village. Had to sell off Eric's granny's grotty bungalow so she could buy this shop. Laura had no idea how difficult it was for some people.

Sharon worked harder too, getting up before dawn to sort the papers and having to keep the shop open into the evening to make the most of what could be a precarious living. No, the likes of Laura, born with a silver spoon in her mouth, had no idea how the other half lived.

Both had been born and brought up in Melton too. Went to the same school, the comprehensive in town. Different years, of course. Sharon sniffed. Turning forty had certainly made her revaluate her life. For some while now her thoughts had dwelt on her place in society and found it sadly lacking. Because she knew exactly why people treated her differently to Saint Laura. It was because she'd come off the council estate. Pure and simple. Despite taking action to improve her status in life, she found that people didn't forget. Not in places like this.

Maybe she should have moved away to rid herself of the background that had its claws so deeply embedded in her, but the shop opportunity had come up here so why should she? Still, the truth remained that whatever measures she'd taken to drag herself up and out of the life she'd been born into, the locals still saw her as Shaz from the family of ne'er-do-wells that barely held down a job between them. Criminals, the lot.

She didn't miss the uncertainty of that life. Of the wheel-less cars that lived for months on the front garden while her brothers "did them up". Of the change of furniture because something had "fallen off the back of a lorry" which only meant that the item which it replaced had to live out on the pavement for an eternity, neighbourhood complaints eventually forcing the council to remove it. Of coming home to find your (shared) bedroom stacked to the ceiling with dodgy DVD players, or similar.

No, she'd come a long way. Even had an en suite now. The rest of her family wouldn't have a clue what one was.

Sharon refused to have any of them in the shop, knowing their pilfering hands wouldn't be able to resist shoving stock into pockets and prams before arriving at the till to pay for one tenth of what they walked out with.

Rather grudgingly she supposed that at least she hadn't had all the drama that dogged Laura's life. First, the car accident that killed her first husband, Matt. Though Sharon had never been entirely convinced of Laura's innocence on that one. She'd had a glass of wine before she got behind that steering wheel after all, and while Sharon wasn't one to cast aspersions, that was a fact. One it was hard to get away from. Sharon knew all the details of the case because she'd sat through the court proceedings, obviously there as any pillar of the community should be, to support Laura. Still, it had to be said she'd been surprised when Laura had got off and had felt a certain sense of anti-climax if she was being honest.

Then Laura had lost her mother in dramatic fashion, bursting a blood vessel while on horseback. What a way to go. But that was the thing with these dreadful horsey women, they never knew when to stop.

And now this. Her second husband, Sebastian, charged with four murders and one attempted murder.

Shocking.

It appeared as though Laura had no control whatsoever over what went on in her home. Something Sharon found unbelievable.

It wouldn't have happened under her roof, that's all she knew. Not with her Eric. As solid as they came, he was. And reliable. He wouldn't be sneaking off to have sex with the young daughter of a friend. Disgusting, that's what that was. What was it about men and their urges? Animals, the lot of them. Sharon shook her head.

No, when it came to sex, she and Eric had worked it out years ago. When Daisy, their only daughter, had been born, Sharon had decided that was enough interruption to her trying to make something of her life and simply said to Eric that since no further procreation was required (she'd looked that word up, remembered being proud of being able to use it), since no further procreation was required, there was no need to carry on with the messy business of sex.

She'd never been much of a fan of it anyway, never driven by need or desire, never over-come with lust, so after using it to get what she wanted, a husband, a child, she felt no need to continue the practice.

She didn't miss it.

Not one little bit.

Plus, it was sex with Eric after all and any sexual attraction she'd ever had for him had been manufactured by fantasies of how he could improve her life. That and her over-indulgence in Babycham and cheap cider.

If you would like to carry on reading *Shape of Revenge*, you can get it wherever you buy your books.

Get Free Exclusive Content by Signing up to the Georgia Rose Newsletter

You have got this far, so thank you again for reading *A Killer Strikes*. I really enjoy interacting with my readers and love to build that relationship via my newsletter. If you sign up to that at my website, www.georgiarosebooks.com, I will send you **some content that's only available to my subscribers**, for free.

Acknowledgements

Ideas and inspiration for writing fiction come from many places and I like the facts in my fiction to be as accurate as they can be, so a big thank you goes to an undercover source of mine who provided me with all the police information I needed.

As always, a huge thank you is due to my beta (test) readers. This time Claire Millington, Katherine Winters, Kathy Sapsed, Andrew Moore, Debra Cartledge and Clare O'Callaghan were exposed to my work at a horribly rough stage as I like early feedback and I thank them for their candour and for telling me what they really thought (even though I know it's difficult!); it informs my way forward.

After we worked together on *Parallel Lies* and *Loving Vengeance,* I was delighted that my editor, Mark Barry, agreed to take on this project as well. I have not made it easy for him and I know he is a busy man. I thank him for his words of wisdom and warning, and for telling me when mine are simply not good enough, but most especially I thank him for his friendship and for the bucketloads of enthusiasm he shows for my work.

There are countless punctuation and grammar rules and I consider myself truly blessed, and mightily relieved, to have met Julia Gibbs who knows them all! A great big thank you goes to her for her diligence in proofreading my work so that the final product is as polished as it can be. Any errors that remain are mine and mine alone.

I feel fortunate to have been introduced (by Mark!) to the wonderfully patient Simon Emery who has designed this fabulous cover and used his mad skills to draw the map. I thank him for his expertise and I am delighted with the end results, a perfect launch for this new series.

My thanks, as always, goes to the incredibly generous online community of authors, readers, bloggers and reviewers. Much to my surprise, finding all of you has been one of the most enjoyable aspects of becoming an independent author and I thank you for your friendship, knowledge and support.

I thank everyone on my mailing list for signing up to find out more. I love hearing from you and I particularly thank all those who have taken on the challenge of being on my ARC (Advance Reader Copy) team. Your early help, eagle eyed spotting of errors and support means a great deal. Let's hope you like what you have just read.

Thank you to all the members of Hunts Writers who read the first chapter of *A Killer Strikes* and provided valuable feedback. And a special thank you is reserved for Sally, Fliss, John and Evie who do all the things I cannot.

Last, but by no means least, is the thank you that goes to my growing family. They have to put up with the actual process of me trying to get a book out and while my grown-up children have now largely escaped most of that, my husband has not. So, Russell, thank you once again for putting up with me through all the times when my thoughts are focused on my fictional world and on getting the work done. x

Contact details

Thank you for reading this far. I'm always interested to hear from readers with any feedback, thoughts or observations they are willing to make. If you'd like to get in touch, or you want to hear about what's coming next, I can be found in all of these places:

My website at Georgia Rose Books where you will also have the opportunity to follow my blog or get some free exclusive content by joining my mailing list at www.georgiarosebooks.com.

I'm on Twitter @GeorgiaRoseBook

On Facebook or you can 'like' the Georgia Rose – Author page.

I'm easy to find on BookBub and Goodreads too, as well as Instagram and Pinterest (although I have absolutely no idea what I'm meant to be doing on those sites!)

Finally, if you have enjoyed reading this, please tell ~~someone~~ *everyone* you know and, whatever you think of it, if you can, would you consider leaving a review? Of whatever rating! You might not think your opinion matters, but I can assure you it does. It helps the book gain visibility, and it informs other readers whether or not to purchase it, so if you could take a minute or two to leave a few words on Amazon or the retail site of your choice and/or Goodreads and BookBub that would be hugely appreciated.

Now, if you're sitting there holding a beautiful paperback or hardback in your hand and you're thinking that request doesn't include me... well, please think again. It doesn't matter how or where you bought your paperback, all the sites will still accept a review from you.

Thank you.

Ingram Content Group UK Ltd.
Milton Keynes UK
UKHW010022300523
422450UK00001B/6